THE GLASGOW BELLE

As the great age of canal building comes to Glasgow, a wild and beautiful girl is rescued from a life of poverty and abuse by the old Earl of Kirklee. Isla Anderson has always dreamed of becoming a Lady, and when she goes to live at Kirklee Castle as one of the family it seems as if all her dreams have come true. However, not everyone is willing to forget Isla's humble origins, especially Lady Dorothy – a haughty and spiteful woman who makes no secret of her fervent desire to send Isla straight back to the slums from which she came.

THE GLASGOW BELLE

THE GLASGOW BELLE

by

Margaret Thomson Davis

Magna Large Print Books
Long Preston, North Yorkshire,
BD23 4ND, England.

British Library Catalogu̶̶̶̶̶ ̶̶̶̶̶̶̶̶̶̶̶̶ ̶̶̶̶̶̶ Publication Data.

Davis, Margaret Thoms(
The Glasgow bell

A catalogue reco ̶̶̶̶̶̶ ̶̶̶ ̶̶̶̶̶ ̶̶̶̶̶ ̶̶̶ ̶̶̶̶ ̶̶
available from the British Library

ISBN   978-0-7505-2689-0

First published in Great Britain in 1998
by B & W Publishing Ltd

Copyright © Margaret Thomson Davis 1998

Cover illustration by arrangement with
P.W.A. International Ltd.

The right of Margaret Thomson Davis to be identified as the
author of this work has been asserted by her in accordance with
the Copyright, Designs and Patents Act, 1988

Published in Large Print 2007 by arrangement with
Black & White Publishing Ltd.

Magna Large Print is an imprint of Library Magna Books Ltd.

Printed and bound in Great Britain by
T.J. (International) Ltd., Cornwall, PL28 8RW

AUTHOR'S ACKNOWLEDGEMENT

I would like to thank Sheila Livingstone for all her help with research about the canals, and for her poem *Cargoes*.

CHAPTER ONE

The old Earl couldn't believe his eyes. One moment he was gazing morosely from the coach as it trundled along, his shoulders hunched. He hadn't bothered to wear a wig and his grey hair hung in an unwashed, uncombed straggle over his shoulders. Then suddenly everything changed. He saw the young girl and his heart gave a bound of joy. He knew that his favourite daughter, his youngest child, had died in tragic circumstances. Yet, here she was before his very eyes. He shouted for the coachman to stop. A man was attacking the girl and she was fighting him like a maniac. Kicking, punching, scratching, making the man howl with rage and beat her even more severely.

'Take the whip to him,' the old Earl shouted to the coachman. The coachman leapt down and the whip cracked and curled around the man's ears and body and legs, making him scream with pain.

The old Earl stumbled from the coach. Another few cracks of the whip sent the man scuttling back inside the nearby hostelry. Trembling now with a mixture of hope and confusion, the old Earl asked the girl,

'What is your name, child?'

'Isla, sir. Isla Anderson.'

Not his Shona then? His dear, dead Shona. Almost ten years had passed since that dreadful day, but she was never far from his thoughts. And yet – the same luxurious auburn crown of curls, the same dazzling green eyes, the same defiant, brave lift of the chin. Yes, it *was* his Shona. He felt the knowledge melt his heart and soul. He could have wept.

'Who was that man who was so cruelly ill-using you?' he heard himself ask.

'My stepfather, Archie Anderson. He used to beat my mother and my young brother. He was the death of them. But he won't be the death of me. I'm not staying here another moment. I told him so.'

'Have you somewhere to go?'

The girl shook her head. 'No, sir, no-where.'

The old Earl held on to the door of the coach for support. Unable to eat properly for some time, he had become gaunt and bent and prone to hazy, confused sensations in his head. Nothing the doctor had forced him to swallow had helped, either his appetite or his state of mind. The doctor had tried every-thing from vile tasting toads which had been cooked alive, to copious drinks of goat's whey.

'Do you know who I am, child?'

'I recognise the coat of arms on your carriage, my Lord. And I have seen you and your ladies entering the Tontine for the Assemblies.'

The ladies she referred to were his twin sisters, his brother's widow, the Dowager, her companion and poor relation, and his oldest daughter, a plain, quiet girl. He'd had four children – three daughters and a son – and his Shona had been so different from any of them. His Shona had been full of life and mischief, and an overflowing of love and affection. She had been his pride and joy, his reason for living – until she was struck down by scarlet fever. Since her death, he had neglected himself and his estate and allowed the ladies to have the complete run of the place and take advantage of his hospitality.

Since the recent marriage of his son, Lord Alexander Lamond, in England, there was talk of him and his new wife coming to Kirklee Castle to take up residence. If this did happen, he could see the place being taken over by Lady Lamond. He dreaded such a thing ever happening. Already he had been in correspondence with her about the marriage settlement and had come to the conclusion that she was a hard, greedy and grasping woman who was used to getting her own way. His charming, easy-going son would, he feared, be no match for her. Such a woman would do his estate no good at all.

'Thank you, thank you for helping me, my Lord,' the girl was saying now.

He smiled at her. Dear Shona. He couldn't let her go.

'Would you like to come home with me to Kirklee Castle?'

Astonishment widened the girl's eyes. Then she suddenly clapped her hands and jumped up and down.

'Oh, I'd love to. I'd love to. Thank you, my Lord, thank you. I will work like a slave. You'll never have a servant who will work as hard as I will.'

'Into the coach with you,' he said, just as he used to say to Shona. He had no intention of engaging this lovely creature as a servant. Already he had far more servants than he needed at Kirklee. No, this girl would be a daughter to him. He realised of course that she would not be a welcome addition to the family as far as the ladies at Kirklee were concerned. Already they were in great agitation about Lady Lamond and the danger of her deciding to leave her own estate in England and come to live in Kirklee Castle. The ladies could imagine the disruption this could cause to the pleasant and comfortable routine of their lives. She might even, as the old Earl feared, persuade Lord Lamond to allow the desecration of their beautiful surroundings and the invasion of their privacy by the cutting of the canal.

'The place will be ruined,' they cried. 'And overrun by hordes of rough navvies. It doesn't bear thinking about.' Indeed it did not. The old Earl had seen all too clearly the upheaval the building of the canal had caused across the lands of some of his friends. He had also seen, alas, the influence a greedy woman could have over a good man. His nearest neighbours, the Raeburns, were a case in point. Hamish Raeburn had never the slightest desire to sell any part of his land but his wife, Alice, was determined to do so and she had eventually had her way. The canal was now snaking ever closer to Kirklee. It had started near Edinburgh and now, in the summer of 1789, it had already passed Kirkintilloch and was busy with traffic. Not satisfied with that, it was fast eating up more of the countryside. The world was on the move and he didn't know what to make of it.

His companion's voice suddenly interrupted his gloomy thoughts,

'Oh, I'm so excited, so excited. I always knew I was meant for better things,' she exclaimed, as tears of joy ran down her face.

The old Earl smiled at her.

'Indeed, indeed,' he said, and took her hand in his. As the carriage bumped along, the Earl felt more hopeful than he had for years. Perhaps this bright young child would chase away the shadows that had haunted him for so long.

CHAPTER TWO

Hatred was building up. It oozed from the stone walls of the castle. They all felt it. It bound them together and even included Isla.

For months they had rejected her. Now they huddled indignantly together in the drawing room. All except the old Earl who had taken to shutting himself away in his study to pen yet another angry missive to Lady Lamond, his son's English wife. It was becoming more and more obvious that the English woman who was now en route to Kirklee Castle would make it impossible for any of them to remain. They had a miniature of her and could see even by the stiff face and black beads of eyes that she was a hard, greedy woman. It wasn't just the selling of the land and the encroachment of the canal they were worried about. She would make short work of the Earl's generosity towards the family at Kirklee. Isla wasn't family and so she was in an even more precarious position. That the old Earl loved her like a daughter, she had no doubt. Nevertheless, she was not his daughter. Even he had come to terms with this although he still occasionally called her Shona.

She couldn't bear the thought of going back to Glasgow and the life she had once led. It had been bad enough when she had been a very young child and lived in such squalid poverty in a Glasgow hovel. Once her father died, her widowed mother had had a dreadful struggle to feed herself and Isla and her brother, Hector. Isla supposed her mother thought she was doing something for the best when she married Archie Anderson, no doubt because Archie's father owned a hostelry on the outskirts of Glasgow. The hostelry had been a palace compared with the hovel but Archie had turned out to be an impossible bully of a man.

Poor wee Hector had run from the hostelry one day to escape a beating. He had gone under the horses' hooves and the iron wheels of the morning stage coach and was killed. Her mother had never got over the tragedy and before the year had ended, she too was dead.

By that time, Isla was fifteen and Anderson began turning a different kind of attention towards her. She had run from the house to try to escape his rough groping hands, but he had followed her and tried to drag her back to the hostelry. She fought him with all her strength, screaming at him that it would be the last time he'd touch her because she was leaving and never coming back.

It was then that the old Earl's carriage appeared and the Earl ordered the coachman to stop. It had been like a wonderful dream after that. She kept fearing she'd waken up and find herself back at the hostelry with Archie Anderson. But no, it had become even better than anything she could have dreamt. She had been treated as his long lost daughter. Of course she'd soon seen why. The portrait of his daughter Shona was the image of herself. The old man often became confused and called her Shona but she didn't mind. Indeed it was easy to pretend even to herself that she was his daughter. She loved the old Earl so much and was so grateful to him. Often she'd fling her arms around his neck and hug him and shower him with kisses. He'd laugh and shake his head but she knew it made him happy. She was good for him. She knew it. She had coaxed him to eat properly and to take more care of his appearance. She had seen miniatures of him, and a large ornate framed portrait of him hung in the drawing room and another was on the wall of the tower stairs. He was not bent forward and shrunken looking in the pictures, as he was now. Instead, he looked very grand with his embroidered coat and long, luxurious curled wig.

Before she had been at Kirklee very long, she had him enjoying his meals, and dressing in clean linen and elegant coats and waistcoats. He had even begun wearing his wig. The clutch of ladies at the Castle were anything but loving, or even friendly but she didn't care about them. She didn't care if they thought the old Earl had gone completely mad. Mad or not, he was still the lord of the Castle – his word was law – and from the start he ordered that she had to be dressed like a lady and taught reading and writing, as well as good manners. When the Earl wasn't there, the ladies – especially Miss Esther Nichol, the poor relation – were very scathing and bitter in their talk and behaviour towards her.

'You may look like the young lady who died,' they told her, 'but you'll never be anything else but a beggar girl the poor demented Earl picked up from the streets of Glasgow. Fine clothes don't make a fine lady.'

The Earl's twin sisters and his brother's widow, his daughter and of course Miss Nichol, were all dependent on the Earl. He had not only provided them with a home at Kirklee but had supplied their every need, even their ballgowns and their jewellery.

Isla had imagined they would be as grateful to the Earl as she was but no, they were a vain and haughty bunch who jealously guarded what they believed was their right. She, they never tired of telling Isla, had no right even to have set foot in the Castle. She wasn't a kinswoman, she was nothing. Even the servants treated her with scant respect. She had taken wicked advantage of a poor old gentleman who was still grieving for his dead daughter.

Isla had just tossed her head and laughed and responded to everyone in not only scathing terms, but impertinent ones. She took a delight in shocking them all, including the servants. The family were always complaining about her to the Earl but as often as not, Isla had pre-empted them and told the Earl about what she'd been up to and what the ladies were going to complain about next. When the family came and said that Isla was impossible and she could never be a lady – no matter how often she was instructed in ladylike manners – the old Earl was hard put to it not to laugh because Isla had spoken these very words to him only minutes before the ladies had arrived.

She was an excellent mimic and could impersonate any of the ladies with uncanny accuracy. The Earl had told her more than once in fact that she could have been an actress. He enjoyed having her read to him every evening. She not only read from one of the books from the Earl's vast library, but she acted each of the characters in the book. She brought the whole story to vivid and exciting life for him and not only with her voice. Her green eyes would widen, she would push her fingers through the curly mass of her long, auburn hair. Sometimes at a dramatic part of the book she would stamp her feet or shake her fist or clutch at her chest. She kept the Earl not only entertained but totally enthralled. So often too, she could make him laugh with her antics.

Isla could hardly believe that this charmed life she had been leading for nearly a year might be coming to an abrupt end and all because of the English woman who had married Lord Lamond. She would be arriving at Kirklee Castle any day now. They all felt insecure. Lady Lamond had already upset the Earl with the greed and impertinence she had revealed in her correspondence with him. The letters from her lawyers about the marriage settlement were even worse. The Earl was actually threatening to leave Kirklee as soon as Lady Lamond had given birth to his grandchild. He could not live under the same roof as such a woman, he said.

'If that happens,' wailed Miss Nichol, 'what will become of us all?'

CHAPTER THREE

It was not round the carriageway that encircled the grass plot in the forecourt, nor through the high wrought-iron gates that the pony and trap travelled carrying Bessie and Lizzie, the laundry maids.

The doorway of the stables in the North Wing opened at the other side from the forecourt into a stony path fronted by a giant wall of beech, oak and chestnut trees, and beyond that a deep pond.

The pony and trap ambled along at a sleepy pace lulled by the flower-perfumed heat haze and the soft whirring of insects. Lizzie and Bessie, well trained in the decorum of the house, didn't usually talk much. But today they were hardly able to stop, albeit in low discreet tones. Down the grapevine of the servants had come rumours that Lord Lamond was coming home. That would have been exciting enough. It had also been said however that he would be arriving with a bride and a sister-in-law.

The old Earl had been in correspondence with his son's lady concerning marriage settlements and he seemed anything but happy about the way things had gone.

Indeed, as each day passed, he appeared to grow more angry and morose. His present mood was affecting not only the family, but the servants.

'Richardson her name is,' said Lizzie, who had heard it from the chambermaid, who had heard it from the personal maid who served the old Countess. 'Dorothy Richardson, an English lady of considerable fortune, they say, and never set foot in Scotland before. There's trouble brewing, mark my words.' Unexpectedly, she laughed. 'Of course, he was always a bit of a rake!'

Immediately her hand flew to her mouth to quieten the sounds that came from it as if someone apart from Bessie and the pony might hear. Although it looked as if there was no-one else in the world except the three of them. The back of the house with its terraced garden and pavilions was still visible, its old walls yellowed by sunshine. No movement or shadow reflected the slightest sign of life however.

Bessie knew that Lizzie was referring to Lord Lamond being a rake and not the old Earl. The latter was a bent old man in a large curly wig and old-fashioned clothes. Whereas Lord Lamond had always had an eye for fashion, as well as a pretty girl.

Bessie joined Lizzie in a carefully repressed giggle. Both had had their bottoms patted or pinched on occasion by the noble Lord.

'It's never been the same without him, has it? He always brought a bit of life to the place.'

They were traversing treeless open ground now with the sun bright and shimmering, and the path a mere thread through the grass. The pony, head down, dragged its heels even slower. The two girls, perched in front of the mountain of dirty laundry, became mesmerised by the heat and were silent for a time. But soon after reaching the shade of the yew trees and perhaps awakened by the startled flight of some roe deer, Lizzie burst out, 'I wonder what she'll be like.'

'A haughty kind of madam, they say.'

'How can anybody know that?' Lizzie scoffed. 'Nobody's set eyes on her yet.'

'Every letter that comes from her or her lawyers sets his Lordship in a state. Janet told me that while she was serving dinner the other day, she heard his Lordship say to the Dowager that the lady must be a very haughty miss, judging by her high-handed attitude. They are all murmuring things about her and none of them good.'

The sun winked spasmodically through the profusion of beech, elm, red cedar and sycamore until the pony stopped on reaching the part of the pond where a stream had been diverted to pass directly by the wash-house.

Here, ghostly fingers of light filtered through. Water splashed and frolicked with muted sound and only the occasional shy sparkle, so enclosed and shaded was the spot by the denseness of the foliage. The blackness inside the stone wash-house was softened by the warm glow of the fire underneath the copper. Soon the smell of soap was sharpening the pungency of the mossy greenery and floating lazily in the air. Lizzie and Bessie sang softly as they worked,

For there's no luck about the house
There's no luck at all
There's little pleasure in the house
When the gudeman's awa'.

Eventually, their work completed, they climbed on to the pony and trap again and began their leisurely return to the house. But they'd only gone a few yards when they were confronted by the Glasgow girl. She always frightened them. Indeed, after seeing her dance barefooted one night outside under a full moon, they suspected she was some kind of witch. She'd certainly bewitched the old Earl.

'Out of my way,' Lizzie said bravely, 'or I'll take the whip to you.'

The girl laughed and with astonishing agility she leapt up beside them before they could stop her. Grabbing the whip from Lizzie, she flicked it against the horse's rump, making it whinny in indignant surprise and rush forward. The laundry maids screamed in terror and held tightly on to each other. But the Glasgow girl knew no fear, balancing herself, legs wide apart, as the horse and trap raced back through the woods at a shockingly dangerous speed. It was eventually brought to a halt in the forecourt at the front of the house. Now, the maids burst into floods of tears. If Mrs McGregor, the housekeeper, saw them, they'd get a terrible flyting. The forecourt was only for the grand carriages of family and guests.

The Glasgow girl leapt down, tossed the whip back up at them, ran to the front entrance and disappeared inside. The laundry maids were so shaken, they were hardly able to direct the pony to their proper place.

Inside the house of Kirklee, singing was in abeyance. By silent consent, the Earl's daughter, who usually entertained her elders with a Jacobite song to the accompaniment of the spinet, refrained from doing so. She instinctively knew that even the Earl's favourite tunes would not have been welcome at this time. Instead, Harriet and Esther Nichol whispered in corners of the drawing-room about the wicked machinations of the English woman. Then all the ladies got together to discuss the situation which was becoming increasingly desperate.

There was no changing the old Earl's mind. Isla had tried her best. All the ladies had tried. They all speculated on what their position would be after the arrival of Lord Lamond, his wife and his sister-in-law, Suzanna Richardson.

The old Earl had expected, quite rightly, that the fortune of his son's lady would be made over to her husband and therefore to the family, and to the benefit of the estate. This the lady had refused to do and the old Earl had become not only angry but determined. He would not live in the same house as that woman. So far no-one and nothing had managed to move him from the idea of retreating to Rome. It was a city he loved, having visited it several times when he was a young man. Many of his oldest friends had made the Eternal City their home after the failure of the 1745 Jacobite Rebellion had forced them to flee from their native land. The old Earl himself had been one of the lucky ones. Though sympathetic to the Jacobite cause, he had not come out openly for the Prince during that fateful year. As a result, he had escaped the general bloodletting that had followed the battle of Culloden. But he had never forgotten his less fortunate friends and had supported them generously over the years. Now, as his life was drawing to a close, and with unwelcome change and disruption about to be visited upon his ancestral home, the Earl believed the time was right to rejoin his old comrades in exile. They would pass many a pleasant hour drinking the good red wine of San Giminiano, talking of old battles and the rebellious days of their youth. Indeed, the more he thought about it, the more the prospect appealed to him.

The Dowager said, 'Not content with hanging on to her own fortune Lady Lamond wants pin money. Pin money indeed! Have I ever asked for pin money? What kind of a woman is this? Lord Lamond doesn't seem to have any control over her.'

There was silence for a moment or two. Then the Earl's eldest daughter burst out indignantly, 'Fancy, both personally and through her lawyers, she said that the conditions of the marriage settlement were not acceptable to her! It was both impertinent and insulting to Papa. After all, he'd done much thinking and heart-searching and gone to a great deal of trouble to be fair. Indeed, more than fair, to meet the lady's demands.'

Her companions fluttered their fans in angry agreement. Esther Nichol's agitation was increasing by the minute. As a poor relation with no money of her own, she felt her position to be increasingly insecure. There never had been any worry about this before. She had her place in the family and played a useful – indeed valuable – role and was much respected and appreciated. A talent she'd always possessed of diagnosing and treating sickness had been developed to the full at Kirklee. Her kinswoman, the Countess, had always maintained that she was better than any doctor. Consequently, her reputation as a healer had spread and many of the quality for miles around had at some time been glad and grateful for her help. She had developed her own herb garden in part of the grounds and had become indeed quite an expert on herbal remedies and potions. Her hartshorn flummery helped the old Earl more than any of the doctor's medicines. She could mix a potion for anything from curing the pox to killing rats.

Everyone kept telling her she had a wonderful talent. The only person who had ever ridiculed this gift was her mother. But then, her mother had ridiculed everything about her, including her male admirers. Her mother had ruined her life. She had never confided in anyone about the lifelong destructive cruelty her mother had inflicted on her. Or the joyful triumph she felt when eventually the old woman had died. She had kept up appearances to the last and even shed a few respectable tears at the funeral. But oh what secret happiness she'd hugged to herself as she'd watched the coffin being taken out of the house.

Her kinswoman, the dowager Countess, had been glad to invite her to come to Kirklee and had always said what an interesting and helpful companion she had proved to be – more like a daughter indeed, she often said.

Now, if she was forced to leave Kirklee, what could she do? Where could she go? Gentlewomen like herself had often been reduced to working as tutor or governess to some awful bourgeois family. She might even have to end up working and living in one of the dreadful Glasgow tenements. There, even at this late date – more than halfway through the eighteenth century – the so-called town gentry still lived up the same closes as all sorts of riff-raff. She would rather die than face such an indignity.

Resentment against Lady Lamond grew like a canker in her brain. In desperation she turned to Isla.

'Are you sure you've done your best with the Earl?'

Isla tossed her untidy bush of curls.

'Of course I have,' she cried out. 'I've talked to him but nowadays he doesn't seem to listen. It's almost as if he's already far away in Rome with his Jacobite friends. He doesn't seem to listen to me any more.'

'It's shameful,' Lady Agnes said, 'to see an old man being driven out of his own home like this.'

'Indeed it is. Shameful,' her twin sister Murren echoed.

'Pox on the woman!' Isla said angrily.

'She's not going to get away with this.'

The Dowager tutted. 'It's all very well saying that, but what can any of us do about it? If she's the woman that she appears to be, you know as well as I do what's going to happen. Lord Baxter was impressed with her estate in England but he told the Earl that it was run like an army camp and she was the general. Everybody had to report to her – not only the house servants, but the foresters, the gamekeepers, the farmers. Every farthing had to be accounted for. Lady Baxter said she was really sorry for the housekeeper.'

'Oh dear,' Miss Nichol murmured. She was thinking how the Earl had never questioned the amount of time the dressmaker had spent with her discussing the latest fashions and measuring her for expensive new gowns. The same applied to all the other ladies except Isla. Not that the Earl would have grudged her anything either, but Isla didn't seem to be much interested in clothes or anything about her appearance. Already she'd shocked the ladies by dancing and whirling about like a dervish outside barefooted. Not even the lowliest of the servants would behave like that. Going stockingless and dancing around like a mad thing in such an abandoned manner. It was really disgraceful.

'I believe in enjoying life while I've got the chance,' Isla insisted. Her green eyes sparkling with enthusiasm. 'I not only enjoy it. I revel in it. That's because I appreciate it. I know what life can be like. You don't. Think yourselves lucky.'

It was only now that they realised just how lucky they'd been. Esther Nichol had begun to tremble. Even if she was allowed to stay, with a woman like Dorothy Richardson, it would be like living with her mother all over again.

'Isla's quite right,' she burst out unexpectedly. 'Something has to be done, and if no-one else is going to do anything, I will.'

CHAPTER FOUR

'What do you think of the place, my Lady?' Lord Lamond enquired. 'Does it please you?'

The carriage had taken a wide sweep round to the front of the house where two lines of footmen in royal blue livery waited to receive them in the forecourt.

A shimmer of intense happiness blurred Dorothy's vision. It was like seeing the place through a diamond. The house, its towers and turrets of remote antiquity, its rows of deep, dark windows, took on – for the moment at least – a magical beauty.

She heard herself say, 'It pleases me very well, my Lord.'

It was not so much the house that she cared about though. It was what it represented. Its firm foundations had been laid as far back as the twelfth century. She felt her veins swell with pride as well as triumph. It was a noble line, one of the finest in the land, and she was part of it now. The son in her belly waiting to be born would continue it. The ancient history of the place beckoned her, promising unassailability and reassurance. Until now, she had been worried about coming to live in Scotland. It had the reputation of being backward and bucolic, to say the least.

Certainly nothing she had seen so far contradicted this description. Indeed, the further north they had travelled, the more savage both the people and the conditions appeared. Even in the towns, the hostelries were more for stabling than for lodging. Servants were without shoes and stockings. Coarse meal was served without a knife and fork. Butter was thick with cow hairs. When one glass or tin can was handed round the company from mouth to mouth, her gorge had risen and she had refused to drink anything.

Kirklee Castle looked much more civilised. One of the footmen, resplendent in white powdered wig, bowed and said, 'Welcome home, my Lord' before leading them towards the entrance. 'Well,' Dorothy's high-spirited sister Suzanna laughed, 'one cannot deny it has atmosphere, Lamond.'

The footman said, 'Do you wish to retire to your room to refresh yourself, my Lord, before joining the others in the low drawing room?'

'Yes, a change of linen would be most welcome.'

A female servant hovering in the shadows of the entrance bobbed a brief curtsey to Suzanna and said,

'I'll take you to your room.'

Dorothy noted that the woman's curtsey and general manner were not altogether to her liking. She would require further training in correct and respectful behaviour. This didn't surprise her. She had long since noticed a certain perverseness about the Scottish character that apparently knew no boundaries of class or station.

For the moment it was as much as she could do, however, to follow Lord Lamond up a turnpike stair to the first floor and into what was referred to as the white room. She immediately sank into a chair to recover her breath, but managed to retain some dignity as footmen, after depositing their baggage, bowed and backed politely from the room. Their respect was aimed purposely at Lamond and meant to snub her, she was sure. Well, she would see about that too, all in good time.

Lamond was leaning an elbow on the grey marble chimney-piece and looking very relaxed and elegant in his lavender velvet coat lined with white silk, a waistcoat embroidered with silver and tight breeches.

'I will ring for a maidservant to help you with your toilet,' he said, and after doing so, sauntered over whistling to the toilet table, unbuttoning his coat and waistcoat and stripping off his linen. Still sitting helplessly enveloped in her travelling cloak, Dorothy watched as he rubbed energetically at himself with a towel but instead of feeling her usual tenderness and pride when looking at his virile body, she felt weak and drained. She managed to smile however when he stood before her in snowy linen.

'You are very quiet, my love,' he said as he buttoned his waistcoat and shrugged into his coat. 'Are you well?'

She nodded and was spared the effort of speaking by a knock at the door and the entry of a maid.

'Welcome home, your Lordship.' The girl grinned cheekily and bobbed a curtsey that made her skirts flounce about and her bosom jiggle provocatively.

'Annie.' Lamond smiled in return as he passed her on his way to the door. 'Be a good girl and attend to Lady Lamond before showing her downstairs.'

The moment Lamond left the room, the girl's bubbling brightness deflated leaving an aura of sullen impertinence.

Dorothy was taken aback by such an abrupt change of manner but decided to say nothing and save her energies for meeting the family. In silence she watched the maid unpack the box with her gowns and toiletries and then allowed her to divest her of her cloak and unhook the gown she was wearing. Then she submitted to having help with washing and the doing of her hair. She did not even reprimand the girl for her unmistakable roughness in performing the tasks. But she would remember the girl's behaviour.

Meantime she bore the servant's obvious dislike with determined dignity.

'The cream silk jacket with the hand embroider, please,' she said.

It was a pretty garment, with brown stalks and flowers in pinks, greens, blues and yellows, done in extremely fine chain stitch. It had been especially made to let out as her pregnancy advanced. Even so it was quite a struggle to get into it and the maid's tugging and pushing made her feel quite breathless.

At last, looking fairly presentable and struggling to remain calm, she made her way downstairs. The servant was going too fast and Dorothy did not even try to keep up with her. As it was, going at snail's pace, her feet anxiously feeling for each narrow, winding stair, and her palm sliding along the wall to keep her balance, she nearly fell a couple of times.

When she reached the foot of the stairs, her heart was palpitating so much she couldn't see where the maid had gone and took a wrong turning into the entrance hall where she stood for a few moments in helpless confusion.

'This way.' The maid's head jerked round the door, then impatiently retreated.

Retracing her steps, Dorothy followed the girl along a passageway to the right of the stairs until they came to one of the doors leading off the passage which the maid opened. Lamond rose immediately to take her by the hand and make the necessary introductions.

A frail, grim-faced old man also rose and Dorothy learned that this was Lamond's father, the Earl of Kirklee.

'Madam.'

He gave a half-bow and, she could not help but notice, did not add any word of welcome to his frosty greeting.

Nor did the long-faced Dowager with the cold, aloof stare. The girl called Harriet, Lamond's sister, bobbed a curtsey and said nothing. A petite slim woman about the same age as Dorothy was introduced as Miss Esther Nichol. She had fashionable frizzed hair and was very genteel in appearance.

'Your Ladyship,' she murmured, and gave a very low, very respectful curtsey.

Lamond's twin aunts eyed Dorothy up and down and Lady Agnes said drily, 'Aye, so you're this Dorothy Richardson that's been causing such a pox o' trouble.'

Lady Murren, the other twin, added, 'She looks peely-wally.'

Lamond laughed and said first to the ladies, 'Lady Lamond, if you please, my dear aunts.'

Then to Dorothy, 'Peely-wally means pale and sickly, by the way. Do sit down, my dear.'

Then he explained to the others, 'My lady has always had a pale complexion but a very beautiful one, I'm sure you'll agree. Would you find a dish of tea refreshing, Dorothy?'

She nodded.

The Earl stared dourly over at his daughter. 'You may ring for tea, Harriet.'

'Yes, Papa.'

Harriet was a plain girl, her brown sack dress with side panniers and a beige handkerchief fastened at her bosom suitably modest. The Dowager Countess of Kirklee was much more sumptuously attired in cherry-red and white brocade with treble falling fan-shaped cuffs. The dress, like the diamond earrings and necklace the grand dame wore, was obviously worth a great deal of money.

Despite her fatigue and discomfiture,

Dorothy couldn't help wondering if the money had all come from the Kirklee estate. There was obviously no effort being made to be sensible with money. She could hardly credit the way the Earl had allowed his daughter to ring for a servant to bring the tea. Tea, after all, was precious, an expensive luxury. At home in England, she had personally kept it in a locked casket. No-one was allowed to touch it but herself. And of course only the ladies would partake of tea.

Her thoughts were suddenly interrupted by the drawing room door bursting open to reveal the startling appearance of a girl. She was clutching a dog's lead in each hand and two very large wolfhounds were straining violently to get further into the room. Dorothy stared in astonishment at the mass of dark red hair, the flushed cheeks and eyes that sparkled like emeralds. Her flimsy dress was clinging to her figure in what Dorothy viewed as a shockingly indecent manner. Lamond half-rose from his seat.

'My word,' he gasped.

'This is my protegee,' the Earl said gruffly. 'Miss Isla Anderson.'

Dorothy mentally rolled her eyes heavenwards. Yet another leech drawing on the Kirklee estate. Was it any wonder that the Earl had tried so hard to augment his finances by taking over her fortune? How very glad she was that she had not allowed him to do so.

Dorothy's back stiffened in her chair as the two hounds came nearer, dragging Isla behind them.

'They're eager to welcome you,' Isla laughed.

Dorothy strained back as far as she could in her seat as the animals reared up in front of her.

'My Lord,' she appealed, struggling to retain her composure.

Lamond got up and came towards her, grabbing the dogs firmly by the collar and jerking them aside.

'My dear girl,' he said addressing Isla, 'we are about to have tea. Perhaps it would be best to secure the animals in their kennels for the time being. We shall make their acquaintance later.'

'Very well, my Lord,' Isla said cheerfully and dragged the dogs from the room.

Lamond returned to collapse into his seat. 'It is an uncanny resemblance, Papa. She is so very like my poor departed sister. I am quite unnerved.'

'Huh!' The Dowager angrily fluttered her fan. 'No more than we were at first. But I can assure you, sir, we soon discovered she is not, in fact, in any way like your sister. Shona was a lady, sir, born and bred. This creature's impertinence knows no bounds. She has no respect for a living soul and her behaviour at times is shocking beyond belief.'

'Tuts, Madam,' the old Earl gently reprimanded. 'Do not exaggerate.' Then to his son, 'She is a good girl and much comfort to me.'

Dorothy felt quite unnerved herself. Determined to control her feelings she turned her attention to her surroundings. The drawing room was a comfortable apartment with wood panelling halfway up the walls and a large glass in an ornate carved gilt frame over the chimney. There were mahogany card tables, a marble topped table, six mahogany chairs with stools to match, and an ancient plum velvet chair on which the old Earl sat. There was also a spinet, and on the walls, several heavy framed portraits. As her eyes strayed around the room, they happened to meet those of Miss Nichol. Miss Nichol immediately returned her attention to Lord Lamond but not before Dorothy had caught the hatred concealed in her gaze. She was shocked to realise that indeed, despite the company's smiling attentiveness to Lord Lamond, who was now relating details of their journey, hostility towards her filled the room.

'Where is my sister, my Lord?' Dorothy interrupted Lamond.

He shrugged. 'Resting. Or perhaps she is exploring the grounds. Do you wish me to send for her?'

Dorothy shook her head. The tea had

arrived and she felt in urgent need of refreshment. It was served by the house-keeper, a Mrs McGregor, and a maid called Ina. Mrs McGregor was a long leek of a woman in a white cap with dangling lappets, from beneath which not one hair was visible. She and the maid fussed about setting a low table in front of the crackling log fire with the tea equipage. Delicate rose-patterned china was arranged on an embroidered tea-cloth and polished silver reflected the dancing flames.

Ignoring Dorothy, Mrs McGregor ad-dressed the Dowager.

'There's plum cake, if you've a mind for it.'

Dorothy was keenly aware that she, now head of the house, should have been spoken to first by the housekeeper. Before the Dowager had a chance to answer, she said,

'Biscuits will do me very well, thank you.'

'That's shortbread, not biscuits,' the Dow-ager sharply corrected. 'You're in Scotland now.' Then to Mrs McGregor, 'Let Ina pour.'

When the maid gave Dorothy a cup of tea it was presented with such impertinent abruptness, liquid slopped over into the saucer before she flounced back to the table to fetch the shortbread. In silence, Dorothy sipped her tea and was grateful for its sooth-ing warmth. Nevertheless, anger was build-ing up inside her. Obviously the staff as well as the family were afraid or resentful that she might make unwelcome changes to the running of the castle. Well, they were right because clearly many changes were needed.

In a few months' time, once she was safely recovered from the birth of her child, she would teach the servants some manners. If they didn't very quickly learn some respect and proper behaviour, they would have to go. She had barely finished her tea when Lamond announced,

'Come, my love. I know you are longing to survey your new domain.'

She felt the resentment in the room intensify but she was glad that Lamond had reminded them that this was indeed her domain now.

'You are right, my Lord, but I wish my silk shawl sent for first.'

She had noticed from the moment she had stepped inside the entrance of the house that, as in most great houses and castles, it was cooler inside than out. In stairways, corridors and unfired rooms, at least. In Scotland generally, it was colder everywhere than in England, indoors or out, but hopefully she would soon become acclimatised. As they climbed the stone stairway, she had to take Lamond's arm. She had been suffering with morning sickness which seemed to exhaust her for the rest of the day. Pausing in one of the rooms to lean on the windowsill for

41

support, she gazed out at the back of the house, taking in the magnificent view of the river, the woodlands and beyond them, the hills.

Lamond said, 'A splendid view is it not? But more importantly, the hunting and fishing are excellent.'

Eventually she followed her husband from the room and began to climb round and round the stairs once more. Rays of hazy sunlight filtered through a window sunk deep in a wall over six feet thick. Despite the sunshine, the walls of the tower were damp with green patches of moss. But the moss did not reach the ancient maps on the walls and the portraits of different members of the family who stared sternly down at her.

She plodded upwards, happy now and wanting to see everything. This was her domain indeed, and already she felt like a queen. Nevertheless, reaching the second floor, her fatigue began to confuse her. The above-stairs drawing room and dining room, the tailor's room, even the King's room – not to mention the other smaller apartments – became such a jumble that she felt dizzy.

The next thing she knew she was lying on the four poster bed in a nest of white satin. Lord Lamond was bending over her.

'My dear, I'm sorry. I've been totally selfish. Forgive me.'

Dorothy smiled up at him.

'Are you in pain,' he asked. 'Has your labour begun?'

'Of course not. I'm not supposed to be brought to bed for months yet.'

His eyes betrayed a hint of a smile. 'Ah, but the Lamonds have never worried about what one is supposed to do. If my son wishes to be awkward and arrive now, he will do so.'

Dorothy felt suddenly anxious. 'What if it is a daughter, sir? Will you be disappointed?'

'I will divorce you immediately.'

When she did not laugh or even smile, he gave her shoulders a little shake.

'Why are you looking at me like that? You surely do not believe me? Son or daughter, it is all the same to me as long as you are all right.'

She closed her eyes with relief but she did not relax altogether. She could never relax completely. Some degree of caution always remained clinging to her bones.

CHAPTER FIVE

Lord Lamond was intrigued with Isla. He found she was intensely fond of the animals. Indeed, she seemed to have some sort of rapport not only with the horses and the farm animals, but also with the wild creatures in the fields and woods. Once, he had come across her in the woods hunkered down on earth damp with recent rain in the middle of a circle of squirrels. The squirrels had darted off at the sound of his horse's hooves.

'Och!' She stamped her foot in annoyance at him. 'You've frightened them away. Just when we were getting on so well together.'

He had laughed at her but she had given him a dark look before turning to snuggle her cheek against the side of his horse's face.

'I will order a horse to be saddled for you and you can come riding with me,' he told her.

Then, learning that she could not ride, he volunteered to teach her. That prospect immediately chased away her sullen expression. She clapped her hands and whirled around in a wild dance of excitement and delight. In the dappled shadows of the trees, she looked like some sort of wood nymph. Or a butterfly in her white dress, her auburn hair shimmering in the sunshine that filtered through the branches of the trees. He was accustomed to ladies – even young girls – who had been well-trained to behave with dignified decorum at all times. Isla seemed utterly different, wild and enchanting.

He laughed again.

'I will have a horse ready for you tomorrow.'

'No, now!' she cried out. 'I want to start

learning today. This morning.'

'Very well.' He stretched out a hand. 'Come up beside me and we'll go back to the stables.'

She wore no cloak and she wasn't suitably dressed for riding. Or even for the weather. The muddy earth had already soiled her white satin slippers. He guessed however that neither unsuitable clothes nor mud would trouble her. Later though, he'd tell one of the other women that Isla must be provided with a proper riding outfit.

He felt an unexpected sadness at the feel of her warm young body close to his. So often he'd ridden like this with his dearly loved young sister. He could understand the resentment and jealousy the other members of the family felt at his father's indulgent behaviour towards this beautiful waif. But even more he understood how his father felt. This girl was so like Shona. Not in behaviour – Shona had been much more ladylike – but certainly in appearance.

At the stables he lifted her down and they went to choose a horse for her first lesson. She wanted one that was obviously far too frisky in temperament to be suitable for a young girl's first lesson. He refused to allow her to have it. She sulked for a few moments but then brightened when she met another more docile animal which nuzzled her affectionately. He gave her an hour of his time and promised that he would take her out again next morning for another practice ride.

She chattered enthusiastically about it at the dinner table that night until even the old Earl had to tell her to hush. He had more pressing matters to discuss – namely the building of the Forth and Clyde Canal and the pressure all the estate owners were under to sell their land. This was to accommodate the easy passage of the canal from Kirkintilloch to Glasgow and from there to Bowling.

The whole family was against having anything to do with the project. The Earl made it plain that even though the castle and the estate were sorely in need of extra revenue to finance the many repairs and improvements needed, it was not worth all the upheaval, the desecration, that the canal building would cause.

Miss Nichol gave a delicate shudder.

'Just think of all those dreadful rough navvies overrunning the place!'

Isla asked, 'What's a navvy?'

There was much rolling of eyes by family and guests alike. But the Earl said patiently,

'It's from the word navigator. They are the men who build and navigate the canals.'

Dorothy said, 'I hear, sir, that it is a wondrous piece of engineering. It improves commerce and makes handsome profits for men of business.'

'We are not men of business, Madam,' the

Earl replied disdainfully.

'Indeed, indeed, sir,' Dorothy agreed with heavy sarcasm.

Already she could see that although the estate was short of money, not the slightest effort was made to be in any way economical. Take this dinner for instance for the family and their nearest neighbours, Alice and Hamish Raeburn. The first course consisted of soup, relief, salmon with sauce, fricassee of rabbits, three boiled chickens, nettle kale, boiled ham. Then there was the second course of a roast fillet of beef, larded, with a ragout of sweetbreads, eight roast ducks, and asparagus. Then for dessert there was ratafia cream and jellies, chestnuts, cheese and butter, oranges, confections, apples and nuts.

She knew the Scots had a reputation for hospitality but in her opinion this was wicked extravagance.

Alice Raeburn was now holding forth. She was obviously in favour of selling part of the Raeburn land. Dorothy gazed at her with new respect. Mrs Raeburn may have dressed too extravagantly – her scarlet gown had ruffles, puckers, falling sleeves and such an enormous hooped skirt it could take full possession of a long sofa. But the woman was talking sense.

The subject however began to cause so much heightening of the emotions that

Dorothy turned the talk to more agreeable topics – golf, cards, race meetings, hare hunting, fishing and hawking. All the things the men enjoyed. Golf especially was much favoured in Scotland and apparently like most games in the country, was very democratic. The old Earl, she learned, had lost on several occasions to one of his former servants.

Dorothy was, however, beginning to become worried about her husband's reckless passion for gambling. Far too much of their money could be lost in games of chance and sporting wagers.

After dinner a game of cards began with everyone except Miss Nichol and Hamish Raeburn taking part. Instead they sat together by the fire in earnest conversation. Dorothy's sharp eyes noted Miss Nichol's admiring looks at Mr Raeburn and the way she hung on his every word.

Foolish woman, Dorothy thought. There will be a scandal soon if that is not nipped in the bud. She resolved to have a sharp word with Miss Nichol at the first opportunity. No scandal would be allowed to sully the house of Lamond if she could help it. She tried to overhear what the pair were saying but was reprimanded by her husband for not paying attention to the game.

In fact, Esther Nichol and Hamish Raeburn were continuing the discussion on the subject of the Forth and Clyde Canal. Hamish Raeburn was a modest gentle man, his sober dress overshadowed by his ostentatious wife who was like a ship in full sail. He was of decent height but seemed to shrink beside her to midget proportions. Even his pleasant, cultured voice could falter into a whisper and disappear under Alice's ringing tone which usually contradicted or ridiculed whatever point he was attempting to make. Not so Miss Nichol who had a fellow feeling for him as well as a genuine admiration.

'Who is there to preserve this beautiful land and its worthy traditions,' she was saying, 'if not the great families?'

'Yes,' Raeburn agreed. 'I am not against progress but not at the expense of the finer things of life. And one must have principles, Miss Nichol. I am not a Jacobite, as you know, but I cannot condone the confiscating of Jacobite land in order to further this canal building. No good can come of such methods.'

'I admire your high sentiments, Mr Raeburn. You are a true Christian gentleman.'

Mr Raeburn leant forward, his hand about to stretch out in tender gratitude to touch the hand of Miss Nichol. Catching sight however of not only his wife's disapproving eye but that of Lady Lamond, he thought better of it.

Next morning, Lord Lamond said to Suzanna,

'Isla and I are going riding after breakfast. Would you care to accompany us?'

'Yes, all right. I can try out the new horse. I'll have to go back upstairs and change my clothes first though.'

'Take Isla with you, my dear. I will be obliged if you would allow her to borrow a suitable outfit until she has one made for her.'

Suzanna did not look at all pleased. But she managed a curt 'Very well.'

The two girls rose and left the dining room in silence. Suzanna was stiff with resentment. Isla followed with a careless dignity. Meanwhile, Lord Lamond waited in the courtyard, chatting with the groom about the prospects for the next race meeting. Suzanna was dressed in royal blue and her long blonde hair was tied back with a satin ribbon. On her head was perched a paler blue hat to match her eyes. Isla wore a fawn outfit and a hat with a long curled feather to match. The creamy colour complemented the warm burnish of her hair. She felt good and knew she looked good. She also knew that Suzanna was jealous of her, and hoped the spiteful woman would fall off her horse. That would bring the uppity little madam down a peg or two. She was as bad as her sister. Both women kept trying to treat her like a servant. But Isla was having none of it.

'I am the luckiest of men,' Lord Lamond greeted them, 'to have two such beautiful ladies as companions.'

The groom helped the ladies to mount and the three horses trotted off. It had been raining heavily during the night and the paths had been reduced to a quagmire. They hadn't gone far when another rider came into view approaching from the Glasgow direction. Lord Lamond recognised the man as David Hudson. They had met at a gambling session in Glasgow a couple of days previously. He was the contractor of the canal and also owned shares in it. Lord Lamond had been impressed with the man and not only as a worthy opponent at the gaming tables. In a very short space of time, Hudson had convinced him of the value of the canal and not only to himself financially, but to the good of the country in commerce and communication.

'Hudson,' Lamond called to him. 'Come and meet my lovely companions. This is my sister-in-law, Miss Suzanna Richardson, and this young lady is my father's protegee, Miss Isla Anderson.'

Hudson gave a brief bow of his head in acknowledgement. It was a dark head, as dark as his eyes. Indeed, Isla thought, there was a strange Latin appearance about his tanned face that didn't seem to match his heftily built body. She could see even as he sat astride his horse that he was an unusually tall man as well as a heavily set one. The way he looked at her was disturbing. Surely such a penetrating, searching stare was rude. She decided she didn't like the man. He joined Lord Lamond, the two men riding on in front of the women, their talk turning to the progress of the canal.

Isla didn't know whether it was the distraction of Hudson's presence or the waves of hostility emanating towards her from Suzanna but unexpectedly her horse slipped and fell and she was thrown into the mud. Far from being concerned, Suzanna giggled. Never before in her life had Isla felt so humiliated. She was about to attempt a determined and dignified effort to stand up and remount when Hudson, who had seen what happened before Lamond, dismounted and swept her up into his arms. The swiftness of his action caused her hat to fall off. Suzanna giggled all the more. Isla was furious.

'Put me down at once, sir.'

Lamond had reined his horse round now and was actually laughing.

'Obviously you are not hurt, my dear,' he said.

She could feel the heat of Hudson's hand on her thigh and on the side of her rib cage near her breast. His touch fevered her blood as well as her anger. She gave him a sudden slap on the side of the face.

'Put me down, I said.'

Immediately he let go of her and she found herself sitting in the mud again. Her first unfavourable impression of him now seemed more than justified.

'Oh!' She kicked with her feet sending spurts of mud flying in all directions. She knew she was acting like a child in a tantrum but she was beyond caring. Both men were laughing now and Suzanna was in a veritable paroxysm of hilarity. Lamond however dismounted and came quickly towards her to assist her to her feet.

'My dear, forgive me for laughing. Are you all right?'

Isla battled with her temper.

'I am perfectly all right, sir. I will return to the house and change my clothing.'

'I will accompany you.'

'No, I do not wish any company. I prefer to be on my own. Please continue with your ride.'

She stood waiting until they rode away. Hudson had turned to look at her as she struggled to remount. She ignored his deep, coarse laughter.

One day, she would make him pay for this.

After returning to the house, she washed herself free of mud and donned a clean dress. Then she took the dogs for a brisk walk. Later over dinner, as she expected, Suzanna made a triumphal verbal re-enactment of her humiliation, much to the amusement and enjoyment of the rest of the ladies. At that moment Isla hated every person sitting at the table, including Lord Lamond. The only exception was the old Earl who never failed to take her part. He was far too kindly to laugh at anyone's misfortunes.

She sat in silence until she could bear it no longer and stormed from the room, knocking over her chair with a mighty clatter as she did so. She could hear their laughter as she raced upstairs in a flood of tears. One day, one day, she vowed, she'd make them all sorry. She'd have her revenge.

At first she had nearly succumbed to locking her bedroom door and spending the rest of the evening in her bed with the blankets pulled over her head. Then she thought, no, she wouldn't give any of them the satisfaction of having defeated her and quelled her defiant spirit. She dressed in her best and returned downstairs to flash impertinent glances at everyone and flounce down on one of the chairs beside them to listen to Harriet playing a delicate air by Purcell and then Scarlatti on the spinet.

Lady Lamond was first to retire to bed. Lord Lamond left to play cards in the other room with some friends including, he said, 'Mr Hudson, a most interesting and much travelled gentleman.'

Isla, despite being bored with Harriet's playing, sat to the very last, only returning to her bedroom after everyone else had gone.

Next day, she arose early but not, she soon discovered, as early as the heavily pregnant Lady Lamond. In the principal bedroom used by Lord and Lady Lamond there was a deep closet. Lady Lamond had decided to use it as a storeroom for everything she wished to keep an eye on and lock safely away, especially from extravagant kitchen staff. First thing in the morning she was already supervising the storing in her closet of spiceries much used in cooking and other luxuries and delicacies such as tea, sugar and chocolate.

The cellar too was receiving her attention. She had insisted on a proper cellar book being kept and already had one recording six dozen bottles of brandy, three dozen bottles of strong ale and nine dozen of other ale, ten bottles of white wine and eighteen bottles of claret. She was heaving herself up and down the stone stairs and along endless dark corridors with a determination that could only be matched by Isla's own.

There was no stopping Lady Lamond. She was remorseless and there was no escaping her attentions. In a relatively short time she had completely changed the running of the place.

'If she's like this when she's pregnant,' Isla

thought, 'what on earth will she be like after the birth when she has all her energies about her?'

The very same thought was on everyone's mind.

CHAPTER SIX

No-one had any doubts that Lady Lamond was worse than they had expected. It was as much as Esther Nichol could do to keep up normal social politeness with the woman. None of the others were managing even that, or very little at least, especially since Lady Lamond was poking her nose into various domestic affairs.

She had gone through the account books, had interfered in the kitchen and had asked the housekeeper to prepare more detailed accounts for her inspection. But she was picking on Isla more than anyone else. Admittedly the servants had complained about Isla but Lady Lamond needed no excuse to lecture the girl about her uninhibited behaviour and her mode of dress. This, needless to say, had not had the slightest effect on Isla. Any of the ladies could have told Lady Lamond that she was wasting her time but none of them wanted to talk to her any more than was absolutely necessary. Lady Lamond's attitude to Isla was obviously making the girl worse. Apart from upsetting the servants, she would hang about the old Earl doing little and often quite unnecessary tasks for him, running errands for him, sometimes just sitting at his feet like a pet dog. He would smile affectionately at her and sigh and pat her head. On one occasion, Esther had heard him say to the girl,

'I'm so sorry I'll not be able to take you with me to Rome when I leave, Isla. I fear I cannot afford to, especially now that I'm taking Harriet. Anyway, there would be no room for you. I will speak to Lady Lamond and appeal on your behalf that you should remain here and continue to be properly looked after.'

There was much sarcastic laughter at this when Esther had told the rest of the family.

'The woman hates the girl,' the Dowager said, 'and I'm sure the feeling is mutual. The Earl's appeal will fall on deaf ears.' Everyone agreed. Lady Lamond had been particularly angry, indeed shocked, when just the day before she had entered the drawing room to find Isla in the middle of a wild dance in front of the Earl for his entertainment.

'Stop this at once!' Lady Lamond had commanded. 'Are you a gipsy girl? Is that why you behave in such an indecent and unladylike manner? You ought to be ashamed of yourself.'

She had turned then to the Earl.

'And you, sir. You disappoint me. I thought a man of your standing would have known better than to encourage such behaviour.'

'While I am still here, Madam,' the Earl answered, 'I do as I please.'

Isla had stood glowering beside his chair as Lady Lamond swept from the room. Lady Lamond had gone straight out to the herb garden. Esther Nichol was furious. The woman had hardly been in Kirklee more than a few days and already she'd taken over her herb garden. She was actually brewing potions and administering them to the servants. What did she know about herbs and their medical properties? What did she know about people and the sickness they fell heir to? She was an upstart, and an impertinent one at that.

Esther's cheeks burned and she still felt shaken by the unexpected and suspicious questioning she had had to endure regarding her feelings for Hamish Raeburn. She had been no more than polite and welcoming to Hamish. Lady Lamond had obviously read more into her respect and neighbourly friendship. Only a few years ago, such a creature as Lady Lamond would have been burned as a witch.

Once the Earl and Harriet went away, she would be left with this woman and her piercing eyes and probing tongue. Esther didn't know what would be worse – either being left in Kirklee or having to go, she knew not where. It looked as if neither the ladies nor the Dowager would stay on at the castle.

There had been murmurings about leaving before the woman arrived. The Dowager spoke of going to live with a friend in the Borders. The ladies had thoughts about a flat in Glasgow. Now that they had all met Lady Lamond face to face, their doubts about living under the same roof as her had been confirmed. They would go all right, and probably before Lady Lamond had the opportunity to order them to leave. But even in the midst of their own troubles, they all felt sorry for Lord Lamond. Dear Lord Lamond was so charming. Esther sincerely believed that far from being haughty, Lord Lamond's wife should be humbly grateful. She should go down on her knees and thank God that such a man as Lord Lamond should have favoured her with not only his attentions, but with his illustrious name.

Lady Lamond however was not in the slightest humble. From the first day she had arrived at Kirklee, she had completely taken over the place. Everyone from the house-keeper, Mrs McGregor, downwards had complained to the Dowager, to the ladies, and even to the Earl, all to no effect. The poor Earl had, in truth, attempted to correct his daughter-in-law. He had lectured her severely and only received the cutting edge of her tongue for his trouble.

Every time Esther went into the kitchen, the servants regaled her with more outrages being perpetrated. Even out walking, she had been waylaid more than once by maids who, trembling with the urgency of their anger, made sure she was up to date with a rush of whispers about the latest development between Lady Lamond and every other mortal soul in Kirklee.

In a way, Esther enjoyed the stir. It gave her a position of importance because she was everyone's confidante. Everyone looked to her for understanding and comfort. Strangely it was also similar to the repressed intensity of excitement that preceded some grand event like the visit of royalty. There was the same eager, furtive buzz.

No-one's anger matched the intensity of Isla's emotions, however.

'How dare she upset the Earl!' Isla had stamped her foot, arms akimbo, eyes blazing. 'I hope she dies in childbirth.'

Esther pretended to be shocked. But secretly, deep down she had to admit that she would shed no tears if some harm were indeed to befall the new mistress of Kirklee.

CHAPTER SEVEN

Dorothy overslept but at least she awoke refreshed. For once she did not feel like vomiting and she thanked God for this reprieve, no matter how temporary. The maid, Effie, she immediately discovered, was cleaning out the bedroom fire and her husband was nowhere to be seen. It wasn't any wonder that she had been awakened. The fire irons were clattering and clouds of dust were puffing about, making Dorothy struggle up coughing and in a panic of concern for the white furnishings.

'Stop that at once,' she choked out.

The girl looked round, sour-mouthed. 'The fires have got to be done.'

'Not like that. You'll ruin the curtains and covers.'

'The fires have got to be done.'

Dorothy took a deep breath.

'Effie, go and fetch the housekeeper, please.'

'She'll be far too busy to come trailing away up here just now.'

Dorothy got out of bed with as much dignity as her swollen body would allow.

'I do not think that you can be aware,

Effie, that I am the mistress of this house now.'

'What did you say,' she demanded sharply when the girl muttered something under her breath.

'Nothing.'

Dorothy made a mental note that the maid Effie would be one to be dismissed along with the rough and impertinent Annie. Meantime she said to the girl,

'All right. I have given you an order. I am waiting for it to be obeyed.'

'Mrs McGregor won't be pleased.'

'I don't care a fig whether Mrs McGregor is pleased or not. Go and fetch her.'

'Oh well.'

Sulkily Effie slouched from the room, leaving Dorothy feeling depressed rather than victorious. So much dislike was very hard to bear, especially when she was so handicapped by her condition. With a sigh she told herself that there was naught to do, for the moment at least, but endure. Wrapping a loose robe around herself, she eased her body into a chair over by the window to await the arrival of the housekeeper. It was then that she noticed that her beautiful cream silk gown and her favourite embroidered jacket she had been wearing the day before were lying on the floor near the fireplace. They were splattered with dust and ashes. It was really too much. Oh, she would have to go all

right. The thought didn't made Dorothy feel
any better. The girl's odious and spiteful
behaviour hurt her deeply. She struggled for
control, her lips quivering over recited
prayers. Had she been her normal self, it
would have been different. At the moment,
however, she was at an appalling disadvantage. She willed herself not to feel sick.

She wondered where Lamond was and
longed for his protection and support. She
gazed at the white window curtains gently
undulating in the flower-scented breeze from
the open window and took a deep breath.

Footsteps were beating an angry tattoo in
the passage outside. Then the door burst
open and Mrs McGregor strode across the
room to tower above her. Dorothy reckoned
the woman must be over six feet tall.

'Sit down, Mrs McGregor,' she said.

The woman sat down without thinking,
concentrating as she was on her fury which
exploded with the words, 'What's the
meaning of this?'

'What indeed?' Dorothy said. 'That is
exactly what I would wish you to explain,
Mrs McGregor. Is it any wonder that the
maids do not know how to behave when the
housekeeper is in ignorance.'

'I beg your pardon, Madam!'

'And so you should, Mrs McGregor,'
Dorothy said, purposely taking the impudent question as a statement of fact. 'You did

not know to knock at a bedroom door and await a reply before you entered. However you know now and in future I will expect you to behave correctly in this and in all other matters, so that you can be a proper example to the maids. Is that perfectly clear?'

In the minute's silence, the veins on Mrs McGregor's neck swelled and palpitated with resentment. Dorothy's eyes did not waver.

'Well?' she said.

'Yes.'

'Yes, your Ladyship.'

'Yes, your Ladyship.'

'No, do not go yet, Mrs McGregor. Where is Effie?'

'Downstairs.'

'And what is she doing downstairs?'

After a moment's hesitation, the older woman said, 'I sent her to fetch in more logs, your Ladyship.'

'Indeed? Well, now you can send her back up here. First of all you will severely reprimand her for the disgraceful mess she has made in this room, and especially of my clothes. Then you will instruct her in the proper method of cleaning out fireplaces. You will also send another maid to assist me with my toilet. Now you may go.'

The woman rose stiff as a sword and left the room.

Once safely on her own again, Dorothy

closed her eyes and tried to relax but failed. For one thing the baby inside her kept kicking and moving restlessly about. Equally restless, she hauled herself from the chair and went over to peer through the window. It looked out on the back of the house and afforded a glimpse of the terraced garden.

It looked beautiful, a peaceful hollow sheltered by a high wall of trees and bushes. Sunshine was held there undisturbed, a golden haze shimmering over flowers. She leaned her brow against the windowpane, hypnotised by the scene and the faint sleepy humming of bees.

Suddenly she caught a glimpse of two riders coming along the path at the other side of the trees. She adjusted her line of vision in an attempt to see them again but the trees kept obscuring her view. Soon she caught the sounds of laughter echoing up through the clean air. She recognised first her sister's laughter. It had an effervescent surprised quality. Then she heard the sensual, slightly nasal sound that undoubtedly came from Lord Lamond.

Suspicion swept over her like a giant wave and as always when such feeling assailed her, she struggled to keep her head and not allow herself to go under. She told herself not to be stupid, she told herself it was reprehensible – even wicked – to harbour so many suspicions. No matter how desperately she struggled, she could never quite cleanse herself of them.

She fretted now to get downstairs and outside to see what was happening. Where was the servant who was supposed to come and help her to get dressed and made presentable? It was wickedly perverse of the creature to take such a long time.

Her reflection in the large glass over the chimney did the opposite of appeasing her. Her black hair was tangled over her head and round her shoulders. Her pale face – paler than it had ever been – would have made her wraith-like except for the solid appearance of her protruding belly and the black beads of her eyes.

When the servant did come, it was no comfort to discover it to be Annie, who had been so rough with her toilet the previous day. Dorothy submitted in grim silence to the woman's treatment, vowing to herself that she would have her revenge all in due course. Now she was just impatient to get downstairs.

The corridor outside was long and quiet. The windows along one side allowed only watery light to point to the line of doors along the opposite side. The passage was dark, but it was the rich darkness of ancient wood.

Dorothy snatched a few moments to admire it and imagine all the famous men and women who had trod these polished boards. Lamond had mentioned the King's room. As far as she remembered, it was the one at the end of the first floor corridor. She could easily imagine, she thought wryly, the regal-looking Dowager insisting that nothing less than the King's room was good enough for her.

'Are you all right?' Lamond's sudden appearance startled her.

'Yes. Why?'

He smiled and put an affectionate arm around her shoulder.

'Your beautiful sister worries about you.'

It was his use of the word 'beautiful' that brought the dark suspicions scuttling back. Concentrating on her battle with them, she allowed herself to be led downstairs.

In the drawing room, Suzanna came gliding across towards her, the sun glinting on her pale blonde hair.

'You look more rested today, sister,' she said. 'You don't look nearly so fatigued as you did last night.'

Dorothy smiled.

'I am completely recovered, I am glad to say.'

Lamond was settling himself at one of the card tables.

'Would you care to join me for a game, Dorothy?'

She shook her head. 'Not at the moment.'

He cocked his head at her sister. 'Suzanna?'

Suzanna hurried across to join him. 'What is it to be?' she asked, smiling and fluttering her eyelashes at Lamond in what Dorothy regarded as a flirtatious manner. She wondered if she ought to speak to Suzanna in private about her only too obvious admiration for Lord Lamond, who was looking even more handsome than usual in his slim-fitting breeches and coat and waistcoat in fawn wool cloth with silver thread and spangles. Her attention was suddenly diverted, however, by the Dowager's voice addressing her.

'What's this I hear about you upsetting Mrs McGregor?'

Dorothy stared at the old countess in icy silence. She succeeded in discomfiting her, by surprise more than anything else – more than if she'd spoken.

'Well?' the Dowager insisted irritably. 'Has the cat got your tongue? When I ask a question, I expect an answer.'

Still Dorothy did not speak and Lady Murren said, 'Didn't I tell you she seemed odd?'

'Don't worry about their sharp tongues, my love,' Lamond said. 'They are the same with everyone.'

'Don't you worry, my Lord,' Dorothy said. 'My tongue is a match for anyone's.'

Lamond smiled to himself. Right from the

start he had been amused as well as intrigued by Dorothy's haughty stare and knife-edged tongue. He'd seen strong men as well as women flinch before her.

'Of that, Madam, I can have no doubt,' growled the old Earl, sitting like a king enthroned on the striped green and gold armchair by the fire, under a massive portrait of one of his ancestors.

Dorothy flicked him a haughty glance. She had tried to be polite, she had tried to be pleasing, but obviously nothing was going to change the family's hostile attitude towards her. She was beginning to think that she had been patient long enough.

Despite his hollow cheeks and eyes sunk in skin like wrinkled brown parchment, the old Earl's appearance was still awe-inspiring. His bob wig was now immaculately powdered and the presence and dignity of generations of power and rank was like a cloak around him. Nevertheless, Dorothy was not afraid of him, or any of them.

The Dowager spoke again. 'We can no longer blame your ill-temper on your long journey. You have had more than enough time to recover from that.'

'It was certainly most fatiguing,' Dorothy said calmly.

'I have made that journey many times with no complaint, and without the servants having to suffer.'

Dorothy gave her a thin smile.

'If you are so prodigiously fond of the journey, Madam, you should make it again. I'm sure that the Earl would be glad of your company on his way to Rome.'

'I do what I choose, Madam, and I do not choose to go to Rome.'

'Ah well, if you choose to remain for the time being at Kirklee, I know you will be wise enough to realise a house cannot have two mistresses.'

The Earl said coldly, 'Do you realise, Madam, that Mrs McGregor has been with us at Kirklee for nigh on twenty years?'

'If that is so, it would appear, sir, that she is a mighty slow learner.'

Rising with difficulty but with dignity, she added, 'I'm going to take the air now, if you will excuse me.'

'Do you wish me to accompany you?' Lamond asked.

'Let me come with you.' Suzanna rose, but Dorothy shook her head. 'No, continue with your game. I would prefer to be alone.'

The atmosphere in the room was too oppressive and she was too restless and upset to carry on a friendly conversation now, even with Lamond or Suzanna. All she wanted was for her pregnancy to be over, to present her Lord with an heir to continue his line and to be fit and well so that she could put a few people in their place. Some of them in a place as far away from Kirklee as possible!

Thankfully she left the house. The breeze was making the branches of trees gently nod, but she could scarcely hear a sound. Her ruffled spirits soothed, and she smiled to herself. As she walked round the side of the house, she followed the tree-lined path – and what trees they were, trees fit to bow their heads at the sight of nobility. On her right was a large beech which she was sure must be twelve feet in girth. On the left was the most massive noble silver fir she'd ever set eyes on. Masses of rhododendron bushes crowded in on either side of her as she strolled along the path.

By the time she had reached the clear gurgling water at the other end, she had become tired and had to sit down on a fallen tree to rest. It was while she was sitting that she was startled by the sound of loud wailing and sobbing.

Dorothy rose and picked her way through the trees and the long damp grass alongside the river. She had only taken a few steps when she saw the prostrate form of Isla. The girl was stretched out on the grass, obviously oblivious of the dampness. She was howling and weeping and thrashing about in an alarming manner. She appeared totally grief-stricken and distressed. Such a naked display of emotion made Dorothy shrink back with embarrassment. She didn't know whether to

71

make her presence known or to slip quietly away. Curiosity won.

'What on earth ails you?' she queried loudly, in an effort to make herself heard above the terrible commotion.

Isla scrambled to her feet, cheeks blazing.

'How dare you spy on me?'

'Do not address me in that impertinent tone, Miss. I am out taking the air as I am perfectly entitled to do. What are you doing?'

'You wouldn't understand,' Isla said wiping at her wet face with the skirt of her dress.

'No, I certainly would not. There is no excuse for such outrageous and uncontrolled behaviour. I leave you to pull yourself decently together, before you return to the house.'

With that she turned away from the dishevelled girl and retraced her steps back to the castle.

The encounter had upset her but only because she had a horror of displays of emotion. She never allowed herself to indulge in anything that might reveal her feelings. If she ever did betray what she felt, it was done in the coolest and most controlled manner. She had always been like that. She had never even shed tears after the death of her mother and father, although she had felt their loss most deeply. She had hated and resented her aunt who had become her guardian but she had always managed to remain polite and civil to the woman, albeit an icy civility.

So caught up was she in her thoughts that she didn't realise she was walking quite quickly. By the time she got to the big iron-studded door to the house, she suddenly became aware that not only was she breath-less, but she was in pain. She rattled the knocker and the noise reverberated through the flagstoned corridors.

In a few seconds, the door was opened by Annie. Dorothy pushed roughly past her. All she wanted was to get to her bedroom and the comfort of her bed. She only reached the foot of the winding tower stairway, however, when she had to lean against the damp stone wall, clutching at her belly.

It was then Esther Nichol appeared.

'Annie,' she called to the maid, 'help me get Lady Lamond upstairs to her room.'

With both women supporting her, Doro-thy managed to climb the stairs. Once she was safely into the bedroom, and had been assisted none too gently by Annie onto the bed, Esther Nichol said,

'Would you like me to make you some raspberry leaf tea? It will help you.'

Dorothy hesitated. Then she said, some-what grudgingly Esther thought,

'Very well.'

Esther left the room feeling a simmer of

resentment. When she reached the outside landing, Lady Lamond called out,

'There's no need to alarm Lord Lamond or my sister at this stage. I can't abide fuss. Just bring the tea and make sure that it's only the raspberry leaf. I do not wish any other herb added to it.'

Esther's resentment came to the boil. Then, passing the lower drawing room, she caught a glimpse through the open door of Lord Lamond and Lady Lamond's sister laughing and chatting together. She caught the flirtatious look that Suzanna was giving his Lordship and she smiled grimly to herself. There might be trouble brewing there for the high and mighty Lady Lamond. She enjoyed a feeling of righteous satisfaction at the thought.

CHAPTER EIGHT

Both Lord Lamond and David Hudson agreed, as they rode in a leisurely fashion towards Glasgow, that they were living in momentous times. There had been the war in America, ending in bitter defeat and humiliation for Britain. George Washington had been proclaimed as America's first President. Now there was revolution in France. Only recently the Royal Mail coach had brought news of the storming of the Bastille.

'I fear for the King's life,' Lamond said.

'Perhaps the end will justify the means.'

Lamond looked more surprised than shocked at his companion's comment. 'Are you a revolutionary?'

'I believe in freedom and democracy, if that makes me a revolutionary.'

'You are fortunate then that you live in a law-abiding, democratic country and enjoy the freedom to express such opinions.'

Hudson smiled. 'You know as well as I do my Lord that in this country freedom and democracy are mere words.'

'We are both free men.'

'My Lord,' Hudson gave him a sarcastic glance, 'you can vote but I can not. Glasgow, Renfrew, Rutherglen and Dumbarton share one member of parliament and he was voted in by a group of four men – one from each of the councils.'

'Surely that is fair enough?'

'In towns only members of the council having a vote? No, it certainly is not, sir. Anyway the Scottish members always vote as the English Prime Minister tells them to and I'm sure they are well bribed to do so. They are no good to anyone but themselves.' His lip curled in disgust. 'The situation is so absurd, sir, that in Bute the Sheriff was the only voter, and he elected himself to Parliament.'

Lamond laughed.

'You take life too seriously, Hudson. And it is your good fortune that I do not. I could have you hanged for holding such dangerous opinions. Thankfully, sir, I am more interested in good fellowship and an honest wager than the running of the country. I therefore choose to ignore your revolutionary ideas so that we may continue our spirited rivalry at the gambling table.'

Hudson grinned.

'Even when I give your lordship a beating?'

'Only with a hand of cards. You cross me in any other way at your peril. I have not the slightest doubt that I am a better shot than you. Another of the advantages of my class, Hudson. I am much practised in hunting and shooting.'

'I have more sense than to dispute that, sir.'

'You are a Glasgow man, I take it?'

'Born and bred.'

'I know little of the place and must depend on your knowledge. I have been schooled in England and then I went on the Grand Tour. Indeed I know Paris, Vienna or Madrid better than I know Glasgow or Edinburgh.'

Hudson shrugged.

'The gambling establishments here cannot

compete with those in Paris. But I think you'll find the one in Ingram Street adequate enough.'

As they rode on, Hudson's mind still lingered on Lamond's last question. He had been born in Glasgow but his parents had been country landowners on a small scale but enough, he had been told, to afford them a comfortable life with servants to attend to their every need. His father's downfall had been his loyalty to the Jacobite cause. He had fought for Prince Charlie and after the defeat at Culloden, he had been one of the fortunate ones who had escaped abroad. For a few years his mother and father travelled from country to country until eventually, after the death of his father, his mother returned to Glasgow to live with her sister and her husband. There it was discovered that she was pregnant and so in 1760, he had been born. He had lived in Glasgow in comparative comfort for some years. His uncle had been one of the so-called tobacco lords, whose fortune eventually enabled him to build a mansion for his family. That same uncle had sent Hudson over to America to learn the business, and to European countries too. But Hudson soon realised that the great days of the tobacco trade were already over.

After his aunt and uncle died and he inherited their house and land, he'd seized the opportunity of investing in the future. As he saw it, the future lay in the building of the canals. It was a decision he had never regretted. But deep down, despite all his own prosperity and success, Hudson always harboured a bitterness against the system that had not only made his father an exile with a price on his head, but had confiscated his land. More land than even his uncle had ever owned.

He had no time for the present aristocratic landowners and the gentry. At least his father had principles. He had been willing to risk everything to fight for what he believed in. Hudson always felt a great sadness when he thought of his father. He wished he'd known him. Personally he cared nothing for royalty – whether it was 'Bonnie Prince Charlie' or 'Mad King George'.

His feelings had mellowed somewhat with age and experience. He'd learned that the so-called quality weren't all cruel, heartless oppressors of the poor. The old Earl of Kirklee for instance was a kind man much beloved by all his servants and tenants. His son was perhaps not of the same calibre as the father, but so far Hudson had found him likable enough.

At twenty-nine, Lamond and Hudson were the same age but, apart from their enjoyment of the gaming tables, that was where the similarity ended. Hudson was of a more serious turn of mind than his Lordship, who did not seem to concern himself with any seriousness about anything. Their differences were mirrored in their appearance. Hudson was dressed in a white shirt with a high collar, a black coat and black-brimmed hat, cream waistcoat and breeches, and high black boots. Lamond sported a long, gaily embroidered coat with gold lace and flowers in natural colours. His ruffled shirt was of finest linen, his cravat of expensive lace. His shoes which were of finest tanned leather were almost covered by outsize silver buckles.

The fact that they had become friends could only be attributed – or at least was attributed by some – to the fact that David Hudson enjoyed a challenge and was as keen a gambler as the noble Lord. Lamond simply enjoyed life, his easy-going attitude, allied to his natural charm, made him a very agreeable companion.

They had reached the gambling house and were at a tense stage of a game when a rider from Kirklee arrived to breathlessly inform his Lordship that his lady had gone into labour.

Lamond dismissed the man from the room with a wave of his elegant hand and without raising his eyes from his cards declared,

'Splendid, splendid!'

'Aren't you leaving to be with her?'

Hudson asked, knowing full well what the answer would be.

'Certainly not, sir. Neither you, nor any woman, will divert me from my game.'

Hudson shrugged.

'So be it.'

CHAPTER NINE

Lady Lamond gave birth to a girl. It had been a difficult birth made all the worse when it was discovered that the child was a daughter and not a son. Dorothy was well aware that a daughter could be a lifelong drain on the family resources. She was hardly recovered from the birth when she began to consider how she must one day find the girl a wealthy husband. The child was called Theresa. The twin sisters, Lady Agnes and Lady Murren, only waited to see her and showed their obvious disappointment that Lady Lamond had failed to produce a son, before taking their leave of Kirklee.

Esther had missed the ladies when they left and sobbed harshly into her lace handkerchief during the goodbyes. She had only been made worse by the ladies telling her to stop her silly nonsense. They weren't going to their graves, they said, but to a snug flat in Glasgow and she would be more than welcome to crack an egg with them there any time she found it possible to make the journey.

Then off they went in their stiff stays and stomachers and linen caps and left Esther bemoaning to Harriet and to everyone what a terrible tragedy it all was. How she was going to survive saying goodbye to Harriet and the Earl, she just could not imagine. They too had only waited to see the child born.

When the time came for them to leave it was even worse than Esther's worst fears. The Earl was a man in his seventies. He would be lucky to survive the journey to Rome, far less ever make a return one. In his eyes was the knowledge that he was leaving Kirklee for the last time and he would never see his home or his land again.

All the house staff down to the youngest scullery maid, all the coachmen, all the joiners and painters and foresters, all the farmers and farm workers, all the tenants and villagers – everyone on the estate from miles around – gathered at the front of the house and down the driveway and for miles along the road to weep and wave and curtsey and respectfully salute and sob out, 'God be with you, my Lord' and 'Safe journey'.

The old man, although bent with sadness and having to be supported by a footman, remained quietly dignified. He had spent so many years here and now the time had come to bid farewell to everything he had held dear. Although he was heartened by the prospect of renewing old acquaintances in Rome, the finality of this parting almost made him relent. But no, his mind was made up, and he turned his back on Kirklee for the last time.

Harriet wept and clung to Esther, however, and said she would miss her dreadfully and she would miss Kirklee and she would miss Scotland. She didn't want to go to Italy, and she was quite sure poor Papa didn't really want to go either. Esther knew without a doubt she would never, never forgive Lady Lamond for what she had done to her dearest friends.

She fled to her room after they had gone and locked herself in and sat dry-eyed on the bed, staring at the door, listening to Lady Lamond's voice outside, an English voice very different from the soft Scottish burr that she was used to. She concentrated on Lady Lamond, concentrated with all the hatred that was in her.

'Don't be stupid, Miss Nichol,' Lady Lamond was saying. 'Come out of there at once and have a dish of tea, and after that you can try and do something with that girl. She's absolutely impossible.'

Esther knew of course that 'that girl' meant

Isla. Isla had created a terrible scene in the background as the others had said their goodbyes and the Earl's coach had driven away. She had screamed and torn at her hair and flung herself to the ground. Now she was racing through the rooms of the castle like a creature demented. It was the thought of doing something with Isla that eventually brought Esther from her room. She'd often thought to herself that she ought to have been a doctor because she was always at her best when she was ministering to someone who was either ill or distressed. She would make a soothing potion for Isla. She decided on a strong mixture of valerium, wild lettuce and hops. She left a jugful ready on the kitchen table and went to seek out the distracted girl.

She found her in the old Earl's bedroom clutching at one of the pillows of his un-made bed and soaking it with her tears.

'Come on down to the kitchen with me, Isla, and I'll give you something to make you feel better.'

'Nothing can make me feel better now,' Isla sobbed. 'You may as well give me poison and put an end to my misery.'

'Don't be foolish,' Esther said. 'Come with me. You have your whole life before you.'

'What kind of life can I have now?' Isla asked. 'What kind of life is there for any of us now that the Earl has gone?'

Esther was too afraid to think about that. Instead she took the girl's arm and led her firmly out of the room and downstairs to the kitchen. There, there was much snivelling and sighing and sobbing among all the servants.

'Come now, we can't have this,' Esther said, taking charge of the situation and beginning to pour her calming mixture from the large jug on the table into cups to pass round all the staff.

She poured an especially large cupful for Isla who was obviously in a worse state than anyone else. Soon the herbal potion had done its work, perhaps too successfully, because by the time Lady Lamond swept into the kitchen, all of the staff and Isla and Esther, who had also felt the need of drinking some of the potion, were silently slouched in chairs looking both depressed and half asleep.

'What is the meaning of this?' Lady Lamond asked. 'Cook, why are you not preparing a meal? Why are all of you sitting around here doing nothing instead of attending to your duties? Miss Nichol, I am especially surprised at you. Go through to the drawing room at once. As for you' – she turned to Isla – 'I'll speak to you later.'

Through in the drawing room, Lady Lamond sat down opposite Esther Nichol. In her usual fashion, she came immediately to the point.

'Miss Nichol, I need a nurse for Theresa. You have medical talents and experience of looking after people. I would like you to stay here and earn your keep in the capacity of nurse.'

Esther was completely taken aback. For a minute she was incapable of speech. She didn't know what to think.

'Must I repeat myself?' Lady Lamond said. 'Do you, or do you not wish to stay on at Kirklee?'

'Yes, yes, I do.' But the truth was she had no desire to stay under the same roof as Lady Lamond, and especially not in the capacity of a servant, but in the circumstances she could not think of any other option and she had nowhere else to go.

'Very well then, it is settled,' Lady Lamond said. 'You will remain here in the capacity of nurse to Theresa. You may choose one of the younger maids who you think would be most efficient in attending to the cleaning and the laundry, etc, in the nursery. Now go and send that girl to me.' In a daze, Esther left the room and retraced her steps to the kitchen. Isla was collapsed over the table, her head cushioned on her arms. She looked as if she was sound asleep. There was no point in trying to drag her through to the drawing room in this state. They would have to wait until the effect of the herbs wore off and that might take hours. Anxiously nibbling at her lip, Esther returned to the drawing room. Dorothy raised a brow.

'Well, where is she?'

'I'm terribly sorry, your Ladyship,' Esther said, 'but she was in such a state after the Earl left – indeed we all were – I gave a calming potion to the servants and I'm afraid I administered rather too much to Isla. She is sound asleep at the moment and I'm afraid will remain in this condition for some time. No-one will be able to wake her until the effect of the herbs wears off.'

'Tuts!' Lady Lamond clicked her tongue in annoyance. 'Well, I'll have to see her in the morning. Tell her I wish to see her here first thing tomorrow before breakfast.'

Poor Isla, Esther thought, with a pity that she'd never felt for the girl before. It was the indecent haste with which Lady Lamond was obviously going to get rid of her that was so cruel and insensitive. As if losing the Earl had not been enough for the poor child. The old man had been like a father to Isla, as well as her protector. Esther couldn't imagine what the girl would do now and no doubt she had no idea either.

She helped Isla to her bed and covered her with the blankets. The next morning she awoke very early and made her way back to Isla's bedroom. She was still in bed but awake and staring miserably at the ceiling.

Esther said,

'Come, Isla. Lady Lamond wants to speak to you before breakfast.'

'She doesn't believe in wasting any time, does she?'

'It's no more than we expected,' Esther said.

'Has she spoken to you then?'

Esther looked somewhat embarrassed. 'Yes, she has. I'm to stay as nurse to the child.'

'And what do you think she will offer me?' Isla said, adding sarcastically, 'Lady's companion?'

'What are you going to do?' Esther asked.

'Tell her exactly what I think of her, of course.'

'What good will that do you?'

'A great deal.' Isla swung her legs off the bed and stretched sensuously. 'Don't worry about me, Esther. I'll survive. I've done it before and I'll do it again.'

Esther sighed as she turned away. She suspected that Isla's attitude was more bravado than anything else. She was familiar enough now with that careless toss of the head and the flashing 'what do I care' look in the green eyes to know that in fact Isla did care and often far too much. She hadn't liked the girl at first, it was true. She had resented her presence and been shocked by much of her behaviour. Now, however, she just felt sorry for her.

CHAPTER TEN

As Isla expected, she was told to leave.

'I cannot imagine any servant's position that you could successfully fill as part of my staff,' Lady Lamond said.

'I am not your servant!' Isla said. 'I never have been and I never will be. The Earl treated me as a lady. That's what I am and what I plan to continue to be.'

Lady Lamond gave a humourless laugh. 'A lady? I'm afraid you're very much mistaken there. You have absolutely no idea how a lady ought to behave.'

'I get on a lot better and behave a lot better with other folk than you do, you ugly, insensitive witch. Lord Lamond obviously married you for your money. You've got nothing else.'

Lady Lamond's pale face turned a shade paler.

'How dare you? Go and pack your bag and leave the castle at once!'

'It's already packed and waiting outside the door,' Isla said with a toss of her fiery hair. 'You'll never have any luck, you know, after what you've done to the old Earl. As for me, I make my own luck.' And with that she swept from the room.

After collecting her bag, she raced all the way downstairs without even stopping to say goodbye to Esther Nichol or any of the servants. She flew like the wind down the wide driveway and never stopped until she reached the tree-lined road that led away towards Glasgow. Half the time it wasn't a road at all but a rough track, pot-holed and muddy because it had been raining all the previous night. Eventually, breathless and exhausted, she collapsed down on the grassy verge at the side of the road, oblivious of the cold dampness seeping through her skirts and petticoats. She was wearing one of the silk gowns the Earl had ordered the dress-maker to fashion for her. Like the wide-brimmed straw hat she was wearing, she had put it on as a kind of defiance against her circumstances. The hat was tied with ribbons under her chin and the gown was low-cut and had flounces at the elbows. The side-panniered skirts were so wide they would have touched either side of a coach, had she been sitting in one.

While walking she had taken off her plaided cloak and hung it over her arm, eventually allowing it to trail behind her. Now she sat, eyes closed with fatigue and despair.

It was while she was sitting there that she heard someone call out her name. Turning round, she saw that it was Lord Lamond.

'Isla, what on earth are you doing collapsed at the side of the roadway? Are you ill?'

She managed to rise with some dignity and look up at Lord Lamond who was astride a restless horse.

'No, I am not collapsed, your Lordship, only resting.'

'But why are you out here on foot?' Then he noticed her bag and looked amused. 'Have you run away from home?'

'Kirklee is no longer my home, sir. Lady Lamond has ordered me to leave.'

Lord Lamond was silent for a moment. Then, stretching out a hand,

'Come, ride back with me. I will speak to Lady Lamond. I promise you that you will still be able to make Kirklee your home.'

'Thank you, your Lordship. You are very kind.'

Her voice choked in her throat but she managed to say, 'You are your father's son. However, I can't return under the circumstances. I do assure you it is not possible.'

Her life would be made hell by Lady Lamond if she returned. She knew this only too well. But she would never forget Lord Lamond's kind gesture.

'But what will become of you?'

'I will be perfectly all right,' she assured him.

'At least allow me to give you some money.

Unfortunately I have not many coins with me but I beg you to accept what I have.'

Pride made her hesitate but at the same time it seemed ill-mannered to refuse. She accepted the money.

'I'm sure we shall meet again one day in better circumstances, my Lord.'

Lamond looked down at her with genuine sadness and affection in his eyes.

'Yes, Isla, I'm sure we will. Until then...' and with a jaunty wave he turned away and rode out of sight.

She trudged on for a while before fatigue mixed with sadness overcame her again and she sank back down by the roadside.

Suddenly something alerted her. She detected a rumbling sound in the distance and jumping up, she shaded her eyes in order to get a good look. The shape of a wagon drawn by a big shaggy-footed horse was emerging through the misty haze. She recognised old Jock McAllister. Hopefully he would be making one of his regular journeys to the meal market in Glasgow.

He reined the horse to a halt alongside her.

'Mistress Anderson,' he said, 'what takes you out this way, and on foot?'

Isla shrugged. 'Now that the old Earl has gone, there is nothing for me at Kirklee. I'm making for Glasgow.'

'Aye well, up you get,' Jock said, reaching

out a rough, gnarled hand to assist her. The horse began clopping forward again. 'Aye, it's well seen what's brought you to this pass, lassie,' Jock said. 'We all know that English woman's reputation. There's stories about her and what she's been up to flying all around the countryside. I'm just glad that neither me nor my wife need share the same roof as her. You've kin in Glasgow then?'

'No,' Isla replied. 'Both my parents and my brother are dead.' There was no point in mentioning her stepfather because she would rather die than have anything to do with him.

'Where are you going to stay?' Jock asked.

She gave a nonchalant shrug. 'I have money enough for an inn.' She didn't add – only for a few nights. But even one night would give her time to think and plan what she could do. She was young and strong and willing to work. Surely someone would give her the chance.

'Will I drop you off at the Tontine then?' Jock asked.

Isla glanced quickly round at him to see if he was joking but he looked perfectly serious. The Tontine Hotel had only been built a few years before and in it was the principal reading room and resort of the Virginia dons or tobacco lords, and other leading merchants of the city. She suspected it would cost a fortune to stay there. She managed to say casually,

'Oh, I don't know. I think I'd prefer the Saracen's Head.' It would be expensive enough but not quite as bad as the great Tontine Hotel. Nevertheless it was the place where most distinguished visitors resided during their stay in Glasgow. It was where the Lords of Session put up when holding the circuit court. She had often seen them as they went on foot to the courthouse at the Tolbooth, accompanied by the town officers with their long halberds. There too in its large hall were held numerous balls and parties. Many a time she had seen the Highlanders trotting along carrying the sedan chairs in which lounged beautiful ladies in enormously high wigs and sumptuous ballgowns. One day and a night there would probably use up all the money she possessed but it would be worth it, she thought recklessly. She'd never seen inside the place and why shouldn't she see it and enjoy whatever it had to offer. She had a taste now for the good things in life and the comforts and pleasures that money could provide. She was not looking forward in the slightest to lowering the standards that she had become used to.

As it turned out, Jock expected her to wait until he completed his business before he took her to the Gallowgate where the Saracen's Head Inn was situated. The meal market stood on the west side of High Street, a little above College Street, and it wasn't too far to walk from there to the Gallowgate.

'I'll manage the rest of the way on my own,' she told Jock. 'You have been very kind.'

'Aye well, take care now,' Jock said. 'There's a lot of rascals and vagabonds going about these days. I've seen the day,' he went on, 'when the only sound coming from any Glasgow house was the sound of hymn singing.'

Isla smiled to herself. Not in the High Street area, she thought. She knew the place well and it was more like a devil's cauldron, especially during the hours of darkness. She began to worry as she walked along the narrow street between the ancient tenements with their warped timber frontages and rickety wooden stairways jutting out from the front and sides of the buildings at all different angles. She decided that she couldn't really afford to stay at the Saracen's Head, any more than she could afford the Tontine. But there would be plenty of cheaper lodging houses where she could stay the night.

Just in time she side-stepped as the cry 'Gardez l'eau' came from above her and a great splash of putrid fulzie missed her by inches. She quickened her step, hurrying away from the dreadful stench. One thing was certain, she wasn't going to try and get lodgings in the High Street or any of the dark and filthy wynds and closes that led from it.

She'd at least try and get something more respectable, perhaps along the Trongate or the Gallowgate. At the foot of the High Street, she was tempted to linger for a few minutes to look at the shops in the archways. One shop was crowded with pails, tubs, churns, butter moulds. Another had open windows piled with projecting rolls of cloth, ribbed or chequered in blue and white, or more homely colours of lightish grey. The next shop that met Isla's inquisitive gaze had packages of French salt, crockery from Holland, prunes from Bordeaux, as well as almonds and spices. Other people were standing around looking at the commodities. Elderly ladies in sober dress were making purchases. Other poorer women in short gowns were issuing from lanes and wynds, some of them to bargain with the shop-keepers.

Isla continued on her way down towards the Cross. From the central point of the Cross, there was the Gallowgate to her left, the Trongate to her right and straight ahead, there was the salt market, or Saltmarket Street which stretched down in the direction of the River Clyde.

Going towards the salt market she passed the Tolbooth which was part prison and part council chamber. It was a high building of five storeys with barred windows on each floor and several entrances. One, at the bottom of the steeple, was protected during the day by a half door with a row of spikes on it. Behind the door was stationed an old Highland turnkey whose green eyes, like those of a wildcat, peered at Isla, making her shiver and quicken her steps.

In Saltmarket Street now, she gazed around her for some sort of respectable lodging house. She eventually found one place that had a board sticking out that said 'Lodgings'. The lower part of the building was hewn from rough stone but above that, there was a timber structure. She climbed the outside stairs. It wasn't the kind of place she would want to stay for long, but it might suffice until she found some means of earning a living. It would soon be dark and she remembered, from years ago, what a frightening experience it could be to be roaming these streets with neither a candle nor a lantern to guide the way.

She knocked on the first door she came to. It was opened by a frowsy-haired woman with a squint in one watery eye.

'I was looking for a night's lodgings,' Isla said, thinking to herself that one night would be more than enough in this place. She could hear raucous laughter in the background and from what she could glimpse of the place behind the woman's scraggy shoulders, it looked none too clean.

'Lodgings, is it?' the woman screeched as if Isla has said something outrageously funny. 'Come away in, come away in.'

CHAPTER ELEVEN

'On second thoughts,' Isla said, 'no, I don't think so.'

'What's up, hen?' the woman said, scratching under her breasts.

'I'm looking for a respectable lodging house,' Isla said. 'By the sound of this place, it's more like a bawdy house.'

'Och, don't pay any attention to that racket,' the woman said. 'That's just my daughter, Nellie, having a bit of fun with a friend. I'll tell her to be quiet, don't you worry. And there's a room in there and a nice clean bed.'

Isla hesitated. Behind her in the street, there was the beginnings of a drunken rabble. Some rough-looking men were staggering about bawling obscenities at a group of sailors.

'Oh, very well then,' she said reluctantly.

The woman stepped aside and Isla entered the shadowy lobby, clutching her cloak and bag close to her body. She felt acutely conscious of her expensive clothing.

'Through here, hen.' The woman indicated one of the doors on the right hand side of the lobby. It led into a fair-sized room containing two beds, a large chest of drawers, a chair and a table.

'I don't want to be sharing a room,' Isla said, eyeing the beds.

'No even with ma ain lassie?' The woman sounded surprised.

'I'll pay you well,' Isla said. She went over and pulled back the blankets on one of the beds. It looked tolerably clean. She glanced around. 'I'll need candles.'

'Aye, aye, I'll bring one in a minute. Will there be anything else you'll be wanting?'

Isla shook her head. She felt thirsty but thought better of trusting the quality or cleanliness of anything else in the house.

'No, just leave me to sleep. I must be up early in the morning. I have much to do tomorrow.'

'I need paid in advance,' the woman said.

'You'll get paid all right. While you're getting me the candle, would you please tell your daughter and whoever is with her to stop all that screaming and shouting, otherwise I'll never be able to sleep.'

'Aye, aye,' the woman said, turning away.

In a few minutes, the house was silent and Isla wasn't sure which made her feel more uneasy – the racket or the silence. She decided not to undress. Instead she lay fully clothed on the bed, only covering herself with one of the blankets. She couldn't even bring herself to douse the candle at the side of the bed.

As dusk approached, she heard the great bell in the college tower proclaim nine o'clock. Soon the rattle of a drum summoned the watch, and the guard chosen for the night would be assembling at their guardroom as usual. The lamplighter would be making his rounds to light the few conical lamps in the Trongate and Gallowgate. They didn't give much light and the gentry always walked preceded by servants who carried little lanterns, although the lanterns only gave out a dim glow through their horn windows. Isla could imagine them bobbing along the streets as wealthy men like the tobacco lords made their way home from their clubs and suppers.

Despite her misgivings about her surroundings, Isla was utterly exhausted and soon fell into a fitful sleep. Some time later, she awoke with a start. The squatting figure of a woman was rummaging through her bag. By the yellow light of the candle, Isla could see the woman's pock-marked face, long straggle of hair and tattered clothing.

'Get out of here,' Isla shouted at the woman as she scrambled out of bed. 'Leave my belongings alone.'

The woman got up clutching at one of Isla's gowns.

'You've got a dress on your back. You don't need any more,' the woman sneered. 'Get back into your bed, or I'll knock you back into it.'

'Oh, will you?' Isla said. 'Just you try it!'

'Oh-ho, the wee lady's got a bit of courage, has she?'

'Give that to me at once.' Isla pounced on the woman, grabbing at the gown. 'Get your dirty hands off it.'

The woman bared her teeth like an animal and clung on with one hand to the gown while attempting to tear at Isla's hair with the other. Isla immediately retaliated with a vicious punch to the woman's face. The woman staggered back, her mouth open in astonishment.

Then she bawled indignantly, 'Why, you little....'

But before she could utter another word, Isla had pounced on her, caught her by the hair and battered her head against the nearest wall with such force that the woman slithered to the ground unconscious. Isla then proceeded to drag her by the hair out of the room and dump her into the black pit of the lobby.

She returned to the room, shut the door and jammed the chair underneath the handle. Angrily she stuffed her belongings back into the bag, wrapped her cloak tightly around her and propped herself up on the bed to await daylight and an opportunity to make her escape.

CHAPTER TWELVE

Watery daylight struggled feebly through the dirt of the tiny curtainless window. It penetrated Isla's stiff, half-conscious state. She had been sitting up all night and now she gasped out loud with pain when she tried to move. She stretched and rubbed at her limbs and soon felt supple again. She tugged her cloak around her and picked up her bag. As quietly as she could, she edged the chair from underneath the door handle. She pressed her ear against the door. There wasn't a sound in the house except the occasional scraping of mice.

Yet there seemed something ominous about the silence, as if the other occupants of the house were lined up in the lobby waiting for her. With excruciating care, Isla turned the door handle and opened the door. Then, feeling her way blindly along the wall, she eventually came to the front door. It was locked. She could feel the big iron key. She turned it and was startled by the loud scraping noise that seemed to reverberate through the whole house. Quickly she jerked the door open and got out.

Down the rickety wooden steps now, not caring about the creaking, rattling sounds that they made. She hesitated for a moment on the rough cobbled street, wondering which way to turn. A stiff breeze ruffled her cloak and filled her nostrils with a terrible stench from the slaughterhouse and the tanning pits down by the river.

She turned up towards the Gallowgate. The tenements were beginning to come to life. Many of the gentry were still living in the tenements. They usually resided in the middle flats with the tradespeople on the top and further down. Beggars or anyone without a home slept on the stairs and in the closes. It was the latter who were stirring first before they were bundled aside or bodily removed to the streets.

Isla felt a surge of panic as the reality of her situation began to penetrate her consciousness. Previously anger and indignation had blotted out everything else but now it came to her that she was in as desperate and homeless a condition as any of these beggars. She felt frightened.

Reaching the cross, she didn't know what to do or which way to go. Her eye caught a hatless man with huge dark eyes and a sunken jaw. He was wearing a thin, torn coat, and was shivering. He moved towards her, one dirty palm outstretched. She became aware of her expensive clothes and the fact that she was unescorted. As a result, she was vulnerable to any beggar or rascal in the streets.

She quickened her steps, at the same time forcing herself to breathe deeply and slowly. She'd be damned if she would allow herself to be a victim. She found herself in the Gallowgate and in her usual extreme and impetuous way, she thought to herself, 'I said I would go to the Saracen's Head Inn and that's where I'll go, even if I have to start as one of the servants there.' She had a few coins left but she was afraid to leave herself penniless. The inn would provide her with a decent roof over her head and who knows the people she might meet there and what she might make of their acquaintance.

If she did begin as a servant, it would only be a temporary starting point, she told herself. She was meant for better things. She was sure of it. She remembered then how she had said exactly those words to the old Earl the day he had rescued her. It seemed so long ago now. But she was determined not to be downhearted and strode purposefully towards the Saracen's Head.

Above the main entrance of the Saracen's Head Inn was a large signboard. It displayed a Saracen, fierce and bold, with a half-drawn scimitar and it was painted in strong, brilliant colours. Isla, head held high, went in through the main entrance.

The hostler came towards her. He was a somewhat rotund man in brown knee-breeches and a yellow striped waistcoat. His brown hair was tied back but a few curls had escaped and fizzed at his temples. He smiled at Isla. 'What can I do for you, my lady?'

On this occasion, Isla realised, her silken gown and plaided cloak had put her at an advantage.

'Yes, I am a lady,' she said to the man, 'recently of Kirklee Castle. I have left there however and meantime, I wish to gain some experience working as a serving wench. I view this as only a temporary situation, of course.'

Incredulity hovered in the man's face along with an uncertain quiver of a smile. He obviously didn't know what to make of her or how to react.

'I am not joking,' Isla said, banishing the man's smile before it had a chance to form. 'I am strong and healthy and willing to work hard. I have a good appearance, as you can see, and I will be an asset to your business. Your customers will view it as a pleasure and an honour to be served by me.'

The man scratched his head. 'Maybe so, maybe so.'

'No maybes about it. Now, do you wish

me to come and work for you or not?'

The man looked harassed. 'But I don't understand. Why do you...'

'I have no need to answer your question. Do you wish to employ me or must I go to the Tontine?'

He shrugged and muttered, 'I suppose you can do no harm. Follow me, I'll show you where the kitchen is.'

The kitchen was a large, flagstoned cavern crowded with hanging herbs and pewter pots. A huge pot of porridge hung on the swee over the fire. A plump cook in a white mob cap tied under her chin was busily stirring at it.

'Mrs Docherty,' the man said. The cook turned a flushed face towards him.

'Aye, Mr Menzies.'

'Here's a lady wanting to get a bit of experience as a serving wench. What's your name, by the way?' he addressed Isla.

'Isla Anderson.'

'Anderson, Anderson?' the cook repeated thoughtfully. 'That wouldn't be the Anderson of The Glasgow Bell, would it?' The Glasgow Bell was the name of her stepfather's hostelry.

Isla shrugged. 'I left there years ago. I've been living in Kirklee Castle as the old Earl's protegee.'

'Oh aye,' the cook said.

Mr Menzies said, 'Archie Anderson?'

'The very one,' Mrs Docherty agreed.

'And why didn't you go there for a bit of experience,' Mr Menzies asked.

Isla tossed him a haughty glance. 'I'm used to quality now, sir. Nothing but the best and The Glasgow Bell cannot compare with your establishment in that respect.'

Mr Menzies looked pleased. 'Aye, well, we run a good place here and there's plenty of the quality visit it. Have you ever been to one of our dancing assemblies?'

'No, we led a quiet life at Kirklee. The Earl was not one for assemblies after his young daughter died.'

The cook laid aside the spurtle and wiped her hands on her apron.

'You'll no' get much quietness here.' And as if to prove her words, a gaggle of girls entered laughing and talking and clattering trays and plates down onto the table. 'Maimie,' the cook called to one of the girls. 'Isla's joining us. Show her where she's to put her things.'

Then turning to Isla, 'You'd better get these fancy clothes off your back. Have you something else you can put on?'

'Yes, in my bag,' Isla said, 'but I haven't an apron.'

'Oh, we've plenty aprons here. Don't worry about that,' the cook assured her.

The girls had fallen silent and were staring at Isla in some awe. But eventually the girl called Maimie said, 'You mean she's going to be working here and sleeping with us?'

'Don't worry,' Isla said. 'I'll do my share.'

Maimie sniffed.

'By God, you'd better.'

CHAPTER THIRTEEN

The Lamonds and Suzanna took the coach to the oyster cellar in Glasgow but on the way Suzanna was startled to hear shouts of 'See the Kirklee coat of arms. It's the Papist. Kill the Papists. Kill the Papists.'

Lamond calmly prepared his pistols as rough hands began to clutch at the coach and heave it from side to side, making the horses clatter madly about and whinny in panic.

'Merciful heaven,' Suzanna cried out in alarm.

Dorothy sat stiffly and silently opposite her, and apart from Lamond, hands clasped on lap.

'Don't worry, ladies,' Lamond said before leaning from the coach and addressing the mob calmly and cheerfully, 'Do touch the coach again and afford me the great pleasure of blowing your heads off.' He aimed the pistols and the crowd, sensing despite the pleasant tone of his voice that he really meant to shoot, melted away and disappeared.

'Do you think we should turn back?' Suzanna said. 'I feel quite shaken.'

Lamond lounged against the cushions, lean and elegant, his corn-coloured hair tied back and his cocked hat fashionably small and tipped forward almost to his eyes. 'One should not allow oneself to be intimidated by such ignorant rabble. You will recover after you have a dish of porter.' Then he winked at her. 'What a bit of sport, eh?'

Suzanna was wide-eyed and, for once, silent.

'Are you all right?' Dorothy asked her.

'Yes,' Suzanna said, 'I suppose it was exciting really.'

Later she thought the oyster cellar was exciting too. The experience in the coach en route had made her feel confident that, as long as she was with Lamond, no harm would befall her. She was not even put out now by the cellar's deep dungeon-like situation. Indeed, inside it also resembled a dungeon and was poorly lit by rush candles.

Soon they were regaled by huge dishes of oysters and porter and were becoming used to the strange Scottish habits. Suzanna was not surprised to see people of otherwise perfect dignity and refinement plunge with zest and enjoyment into the vulgarity of the occasion. After the table was cleared, she was told brandy and rum punch would be served and there would be dancing. The part Dorothy said she particularly frowned on was when the ladies had to retire to another room for a time and the gentlemen sat down again to crown the pleasures of the evening with a debauch. The capacity for drinking in Scotland seemed to her more savage than sociable but on this occasion, before the brandy and rum punch stage was reached, Suzanna noticed a familiar face and cried out, 'Oh, look who's just come in.'

Dorothy turned. 'Who?'

'The Raeburns.' Suzanna waved a friendly welcome and Lamond called out, 'Over here.'

Then as Alice Raeburn's plump figure sparkling with diamonds bore down on them, it became obvious that Hamish Raeburn, following in her wake, was even paler than usual. His lantern-jawed face was like a death mask.

'Oh, Mr Raeburn,' Suzanna said, 'what has happened? You look quite ill.'

Alice Raeburn flopped down onto a chair, her plump, bejewelled hand energetically flapping her fan. 'Faith, 'tis I who need the sympathy. If it hadn't been for our coachman and footman, I dread to think what might have happened. We were set upon by a riotous mob of anti-Catholics.'

'So were we,' Suzanna said breathlessly.

Alice's mouth twisted with sarcasm. 'I dare say you were in no serious danger with a gentleman of courage like Lord Lamond present.'

Suzanna said, 'Lord Lamond is most fortunate not only to be younger than your husband, Mrs Raeburn, but to enjoy perfect health and strength.'

'Ah yes,' Mrs Raeburn smiled sweetly, 'it is indeed a most unfortunate business being too weak to give one's lady the protection to which she is entitled.'

A huge dish of oysters had been placed before Hamish Raeburn by a ruddy-faced girl in a frilly mob cap. Another was set before his wife. She started to eat with relish but he sat staring miserably at his plate.

'No stomach either, Mr Raeburn?' his wife said.

Obviously forcing himself, he swallowed one oyster after another, turning quite green in the process. His wife continued eating in complete unconcern.

The others looked distinctly uncomfortable. They were quickly diverted, however, when they were joined by Lady Agnes and Lady Murren, who had followed in sedans. The Lamonds were staying at their flat for a few nights. The next evening, Suzanna and Dorothy were to join the guests at one of the tea parties and soirees that the twin aunts were becoming quite famous for in the town.

Lord Lamond said he was planning to meet with some gentleman friends to discuss books and politics. Both Suzanna and Dorothy suspected, however, that gambling was the subject most on his mind. And one of the gentlemen would be David Hudson. Neither Dorothy nor Suzanna approved of the man. For one thing they did not regard him as a gentleman and they were convinced he was having a bad influence on the noble lord.

'What I liked about this evening,' Dorothy told Suzanna and Lamond as they returned to the flat, 'was how full scope was given to the conversational power of all the company, ladies on an equal basis with the men. That is the first time in my life that I have found myself in spirited argument with men about books and life, and even politics, and been taken seriously. I found it most stimulating.'

'Ah, but you are a most unusual woman, my dear,' Lord Lamond said. 'Most of the ladies in the company, I am sure, would just be enjoying the oysters.'

They arrived at the tall building in which the ladies had their abode. Neither Dorothy nor Suzanna could get used to the custom in Glasgow for all sorts of people, poor and rich, commoners and titled ladies and gentlemen, to live up the same stairs in the city's tenements.

The turnpike staircase leading to the ladies' house was very dark and narrow. Two of the ladies' maids were waiting at the close mouth to lead them upstairs, one carrying a lantern in front of them and the other maid carrying a lantern at the back.

'I suppose the ladies dare not go out at night unless accompanied by a gentleman with pistols like yourself,' Dorothy said to Lord Lamond. 'Footpads could well set upon them on this stair before they even reached the street.'

'My dear Dorothy,' Lamond said, 'you are thinking of English towns. In London, for instance, one is entertained every morning by some dreadful account of robbery or outrage committed the evening before. Here, however, one can go with the same security at midnight as noonday.'

'Oh fiddle,' Suzanna laughed. 'We did not feel very secure this evening with a mob of ruffians attacking us.'

'Ah, it is different when passions are aroused, especially religious passions. But I am talking about crime. I do assure you, a man in the course of his whole life shall not have the ill-fortune here to meet with a housebreaker or even a single footpad, and a lady could walk along the streets at any hour without fear of being molested.'

Dorothy shook her head. 'Really, Lamond, I find that very hard to believe.'

Lamond shrugged. 'My dear, as you know, I have been in Glasgow on my own and with gentlemen friends quite a few times recently. I can assure you that after eleven o'clock, everything is quiet and silent. Now and again, mostly in the early hours of the morning, one might hear little parties at the taverns amusing themselves by breaking bottles and glasses, but that is all in good humour and no business of the constable on watch, or of anyone else.'

They had reached the ladies' door and the lantern gave it an amber tinge as the tirling pin rasped and echoed harshly within the house. Almost immediately they were welcomed by a happily grinning maid who obviously, despite her lowly station and untidy appearance, imagined she was one of the family. Then the ladies who had returned home earlier bustled through to welcome them. The drawing room was cosy with rust-coloured velvet curtains, gold and rust carpet and a coal fire in the hearth. The lights of the candelabra gently flickered on the darkly polished table.

'Teeny,' Lady Agnes addressed the maid, 'I think we would all like a wee nightcap before we go to our beds.'

Teeny grinned in delight. 'I'll run through to the kitchen and make you all hot toddies. I'll no' take a minute.'

With that she rushed, almost skipped, from the room. Dorothy sighed to herself and thought she would never get used to the behaviour of Scottish servants.

'I heard something very interesting to-night,' Lady Murren said as they all settled round the fire with their drinks.

Suzanna's eyes sparkled as she leaned forward. She enjoyed any titbit of gossip.

'I had a crack with Lady Baxter and she was telling me she was out riding the other day and saw your Miss Nichol.'

'Oh, is that all?' Suzanna relaxed back in disappointment.

Dorothy said, 'She'd be out giving little Theresa the air. I told you she's the child's nurse now.'

'Oh aye, that might well be,' Lady Murren said, 'but as it happens, she was strolling along with Hamish Raeburn.'

Suzanna laughed. 'They must have just met while they were both taking the air. After all, the Raeburns are our nearest neighbours. You can't imagine, surely, that there's any romantic attachment between them? Who on earth could think of Hamish Raeburn as in any way romantic or even vaguely attractive? Not even Miss Nichol, surely?'

Dorothy didn't share in the laughter. On the contrary, she did not find the matter in the least amusing. She would have to talk to the woman again. She had no intention of allowing one breath of scandal to touch the noble house of Lamond.

CHAPTER FOURTEEN

Theresa was taking her afternoon nap. Esther had told the maid to keep herself busy with some task in the nursery, but at the same time keep her eye on the child. It was the time that she usually went for her walk and it had become a habit with Hamish Raeburn to take the air at the same hour.

After donning her bonnet and cloak, she slipped quietly from the castle and made her way towards the wooded area beside the river. He was waiting for her, resting against one of the trees.

When she arrived and stood before him, she gazed at him in silence for a few seconds. Poor man, she thought, with his wispy hair, hollow cheeks and tragic eyes, and always, despite his expensive clothes, so untidy and neglected in appearance. What he must suffer at the hands of his insensitive and selfish wife!

'How are you, Mr Raeburn?' she asked gently.

'Dare I hope that you have still some friendly regard for me after the other night, Miss Nichol?'

'The other night? What can you mean?

What crime did you commit the other night, Mr Raeburn?'

His eyes were strained with the many layers of emotion they contained. Deep sadness, shame, embarrassment, anxiety, desperate hope.

'I believe my wife did mention the most shameful and regrettable fact that I almost fainted during the anti-Catholic attack. If it had not been for our burly footman and coachman...' He bit his lip and shook his head.

'Tuts,' Esther said. 'I'm surprised at you, Mr Raeburn. Do you really think so little of me as that? Do you really believe I would have less friendly regard for you because you, an ill man, suffered physical distress during a shocking attack by ruffians? On the contrary, Mr Raeburn, my friendly regard has deepened into an anguish of concern. Such a shock to your delicate constitution, Mr Raeburn. I dare not think of the consequences.'

'Oh my dear, dear Miss Nichol! What can I say?'

'You can put me out of my suspense and tell me how you feel now. Has your stomach settled yet?'

But before he could reply, a sharp voice startled them.

'Miss Nichol.'

Esther whirled round to face Lady Lamond.

116

'Miss Nichol, what are you doing here?' Dorothy asked. 'Why aren't you in the nursery attending to the child?'

'Theresa is having her afternoon nap, your Ladyship, and I have left the maid to keep a close watch on her.'

'I did not employ her to look after Theresa. I employed *you* to be a nurse and take charge of her well-being. I suggest that you should remember your place and get back to the nursery at once.'

'Oh I'm sure, Lady Lamond,' Mr Raeburn cried out in great agitation, 'that no-one, no-one could be more conscientious about your child's welfare than Miss Nichol. She is a kinswoman, after all.'

'I cannot see, Mr Raeburn,' Dorothy eyed him coldly, 'why Miss Nichol should be any concern of yours. Good afternoon, sir.'

As Esther hurried back to the castle, she was shivering violently with distress and fury. Her friendship with Mr Raeburn – and it was a perfectly innocent friendship, she told herself – was the only thing that made her life worthwhile and gave it any meaning. He was her friend, her only friend now. How dare Lady Lamond interfere in such a high-handed manner? How dare she try to demean her in front of Mr Raeburn by talking about her so-called place? She hated the woman. She always had but now the hatred smouldered darkly, deeply, inside her.

No sooner had she returned to the castle when Annie, one of the maids, came hurrying to tell her that her Ladyship wanted her to come to the drawing room at once.

'She looked white with rage.' Annie who had always been prone to exaggeration and dramatics was enjoying this bit of excitement. 'You'd better run along.'

'I'll do no such thing as "run along", as you put it, Annie,' Miss Nichol said. 'I will walk to the drawing room in my usual dignified fashion and when I am ready.'

'Huh,' Annie said, offended at Miss Nichol's high-handed tone. After all, Miss Nichol was just a nurse now, a servant.

'Please yourself. It's your funeral.' With that, she flounced away.

Esther hesitated about donning the nurse's uniform. She longed to arrive at the drawing room in her best dress. But prudence made her think twice. Lady Lamond had already told her, 'In future, Miss Nichol, you will wear your cap and apron in the nursery and any other parts of the house in which you might be seen.' Esther hated the white apron and cap. It was painful for her almost beyond endurance to wear it and stand before Lady Lamond in the drawing room and be lectured about proper behaviour and morals.

She tried as usual to defend her friendship with Hamish Raeburn but, as usual, was immediately silenced. Only the arrival in the room of a smiling Lord Lamond facilitated her escape. Dear Lord Lamond. He deserved a better life than being tied to such a cruel devil of a woman. As she hurried back upstairs to the nursery, she prayed that some accident would befall Lady Lamond, releasing them all from the misery that damned woman had brought to Kirklee.

CHAPTER FIFTEEN

It had been difficult for Isla at first. The other serving wenches took an instant dislike to her. This was because of her fine clothes and her ability to read and write. More than that though, they resented the fact that she could converse, if need be, with some of the distinguished guests in an intelligent way, rather than the giggly and coquettish way of the other maids. Though she could be more mischievous and flirtatious than any of them when she'd a mind to. Nevertheless the other girls picked on her, sneered at her and called her names like Mistress High and Mighty. They disliked her and no-one disliked her more than Mrs Menzies, the owner of the Saracen's Head Inn.

Mr Menzies had married a woman much older than himself who had been left the inn by a previous husband. It was suspected – indeed most people felt certain – that Mr Menzies had married the old dame just to get a home, or more accurately to get the Saracen's Head Inn. His spouse had a very large nose and a deeply pock-marked skin. As well as these disadvantages, she had a very bent frame and had to support herself with a sturdy stick as she shuffled along. Mrs Menzies glowered at Isla every time she came across her. She had to accept, however, that Isla was a good worker and a very handy person to have around, with her ability to write a good hand and her cleverness and speed at counting. Also it could not be denied that some of the best customers at the Saracen's Head thought her a worthy addition to the place. Even the Provost had remarked on this, and many noble gentlemen had agreed with the sentiment.

Mrs Menzies was proud of the fact that her inn was the rendezvous of all the nobility in the west, as well as distinguished strangers. It was the place where balls, suppers and county meetings were held. All the gentry for miles around, as well as the better-off class of the citizens – lay and cleric – often enjoyed an evening of innocent hilarity and mirth and the opportunity to partake of the good things of life at the Saracen's Head.

Indeed, all beauty and fashion assembled here. Mrs Menzies hovered in the background and in shadowy corners, savouring the sight of blue coats with gilt buttons as large as a halfpenny, white vests and nankeen knee-breeks. She cackled with vicarious pleasure as she watched ladies as well as gentlemen bobbing and flinging themselves about in the spacious ballroom. The place was lit up by dripping tallow candles and brightened also by the brisk reel music from the fiddlers' loft.

Isla enjoyed all the colour and energy, the glees and sprees of the place, although she would rather have been one of the revellers than the person who served them. She would have preferred not to be one of those who thronged the stairs with trays and dishes dressed in snowy aprons and frilly mob caps. But there was the cheerful thought that she would not always be a servant. Temporary or not, though, she still had to establish the toughness of her present credentials. She did this by picking on one of the girls who was most guilty of sneering at her and making a fool of her in front of all the other maids milling about in the kitchen. She lifted up a bucket of slops and poured it over the girl's head. The girl screamed and choked and spluttered and the other girls gaped at the scene in shocked silence.

Isla looked around at them. 'Well,' she said, 'is there anyone else with a mind to torment me? Speak up now so that I don't need to waste time in going for another bucketful.'

After that, they acquired more respect for her and left her alone. Even so, Isla could feel their jealousy still simmering under the surface.

It became more obvious one day, when a very important gentleman arrived by stagecoach from the far-off city of London. There was always great excitement in the inn when a stagecoach arrived. Indeed, it made a stir throughout the whole of the town. The inn boasted connecting stables containing upwards of sixty stalls and was always busy with post chaises and gigs and coaches, as well as the horses of local customers.

The gentleman who arrived from London was a foppish man with a long thin face, rouged cheeks and a lace-edged handkerchief frothing from his cuff. His coat, waistcoat and knee-breeches were all made of matching silk and his coat had flaring skirts, deep cuffs and pockets and on his feet were buckled shoes. All the serving wenches, including Isla, had crowded outside to watch the arrival of the stage and the gentleman's haughty entrance.

It so happened Isla was standing nearest to the door and caught his eye. She didn't particularly like the way he looked at her, indeed she resented it, and tossed her head and returned a look even more disdainful than his. Later, all was a buzz in the in kitchen. As it turned out, the gentleman who had just arrived was the son of a Scottish duke who had been educated in England and then had finished his education by going on his Grand Tour. He had stopped off in Glasgow before continuing his journey up north to his father's Highland castle. There was to be a supper after the dancing assembly served in the tearoom which was situated upstairs from the ballroom.

Invitations had gone out to all the quality for miles around. Including, Isla learned, the Lord and Lady of Kirklee Castle. With a growing sense of foreboding, Isla contemplated the indignity of coming face to face with Dorothy Lamond under these circumstances. But she determined to brazen it out, whatever happened.

CHAPTER SIXTEEN

Lady Lamond added cruel insult to injury. The Raeburns had been invited to lunch. They had no sooner arrived when Lady Lamond sent for Esther to bring the child to the drawing room for inspection by the Raeburns. Esther knew at once that it was not the child that Lady Lamond wanted the

Raeburns to see. Lady Lamond wanted Esther to be embarrassed and humiliated.

Standing before Alice and Hamish Raeburn in her white cap and apron, Esther felt she was dying. She would never forgive Lady Lamond for this indignity.

While Alice Raeburn was cooing over little Theresa, Esther allowed her eyes to flicker over towards Hamish. She saw in his anguished stare the extent of his sympathy towards her. He knew how she felt. After what seemed an eternity, Lady Lamond, without even turning towards her, dismissed Esther with a flick of her hand. 'You may go now.'

Outside the drawing room, Esther had to lean up against the bannisters of the stair before she could summon enough strength to carry the child up to the nursery. As if the little girl sensed Esther's outrage and distress, she began to cry.

'Don't be afraid, Theresa,' Esther whispered, 'it's not you that I'm angry at.' If the child had resembled Lady Lamond in any way, if she'd had the woman's coal-black hair and dark, beady eyes, it might have been different. As it was, Theresa had her father's blue eyes and creamy blonde hair. She even had his placid good nature. It was a most unusual occurrence for Theresa to cry. Esther tried to hush her, but to no avail.

As soon as she reached the nursery, she handed the child over to the maid. Then she went through to her own room and shut the door. She couldn't bear it any longer. She remembered only too well life as it had been before the arrival of Lady Lamond. She remembered how she'd had a personal maid to arrange her hair and help her to dress. She remembered leisurely days in the drawing room enjoying a dish of tea with the dowager Countess and Harriet and the two ladies. Many a pleasant evening hour she'd spent there too, working on her tapestry while she listened to Harriet playing a pleasant little tune on the spinet. The old Earl had been planning to buy one of the new pianos but of course that would never happen now. Lady Lamond was too miserly to spend money on such frivolous luxuries. It had been such a peaceful time and she had been a valued member of a close-knit and happy family. She couldn't bear her life now. How many more cruel humiliations awaited her at the hands of Lady Lamond?

She was not a servant. She had been born a lady and was a lady still. She was a kinswoman of the noble house of Lamond. She always had been and she always would be. In her eyes, Lady Lamond was nothing more than an evil witch who had broken up the family and caused nothing but trouble, distress and pain to everyone.

It was only too obvious to Esther that Lady Lamond had not even made Lord Lamond happy. He was hardly ever at home. When he wasn't out hunting or shooting with gentlemen friends, he was off on his own at every opportunity to Glasgow or Edinburgh. He would be well rid of the woman, they all would. Suddenly, in the midst of her despair, the solution became obvious.

She knew of herbs that could not only kill rats, but kill Lady Lamond. But she immediately banished the thought from her head. She was not a murderess.

She felt ashamed and alarmed at the awful thoughts that had entered her head. She gazed at her reflection in her dressing table mirror, if one could call the old chest of drawers a dressing table. The mirror above it was spotted and rusty-looking. Both the chest of drawers and the mirror had been cast-offs from some other part of the house. The mirror showed her small, delicately-boned face and large, apprehensive eyes. Her hair, once so fashionable, was a limp disaster hidden beneath the hated white cap. A few strands had escaped to trail almost comically over her face. Near to tears, she stuffed them back into the cap.

What had she come to, looking like this, feeling like this, thinking like this? She must remember that she was a lady, a gentlewoman. She must be strong and behave with dignity and think only pure thoughts at all times. But she was not strong. She had always had a delicate constitution. Now she was trembling with such weakness she had to stumble over to the nearest chair and collapse into it.

It was Lady Lamond who was strong. Impossible fantasies tumbled desperately about in Esther's brain. If Lady Lamond had been weakened with childbirth, or had taken a fever, she could have looked after her. She imagined looking after Lady Lamond, and Lady Lamond being grateful to her and treating her with respect. She had always been at her best when somebody needed her.

But Lady Lamond was not weakened by anything and needed no-one. The fantasy of Lady Lamond taking ill and needing her medical attention refused to go away. Esther began to think of her herbal poison again. Not to murder but perhaps just to cause a little malaise?

Downstairs in the dining room, Lord and Lady Lamond, Suzanna and the Raeburns were enjoying baked salmon, followed by rhubarb and custard tart. Or at least everyone except Hamish Raeburn was enjoying the food. He was miserably picking at each dish.

'Is the food not to your liking, Mr Raeburn?' Dorothy asked.

Hamish made an obvious effort to pull himself together.

'Indeed, indeed, the food is delicious,

Lady Lamond. It's just that I seem to have no appetite for anything at the moment.'

'Tuts, that's nothing to worry about,' Dorothy said. 'I can soon put you right with one of the herbs from my herb garden.'

'I'm afraid, dear Lady Lamond,' Mrs Raeburn said, 'it's not a question of Mr Raeburn's constitution, but alas, of his nature. And I cannot imagine any herbs that would be able to put backbone in a man.'

Suzanna laughed with embarrassment and said, 'Mr Raeburn, are you going to attend the special dancing assembly at the Saracen's Head Inn? I believe it's in honour of the Duke of Skye's son who is a guest there at the moment. We are all going.'

'Oh yes,' Mrs Raeburn answered for him, 'we will have to take an extra coachman, of course, for protection in case there is any repetition of those dreadful anti-Catholic riots. I heard a rumour that there has even been an attack on the Cathedral. What on earth is the world coming to?'

Lord Lamond had been leaning back in his chair, enjoying a leisurely glass of claret. Now he said, 'It is nothing that need concern any of us, I do assure you. The ignorant rabble will soon be caught and severely dealt with. I was just saying to Lord Baxter the other day that shooting or hanging is too good for them. They should be sent to the galleys for a few years, or indeed for the rest of the their miserable lives, and he agreed with me.'

'Oh, I am looking forward to the assembly,' Suzanna said, her mind still on more pleasant things. 'I've never been in the Saracen's Head and I hear it has a splendid ballroom.'

Lord Lamond smiled at her.

'I hope you will partner me in one of the dances, Suzanna.'

Suzanna flashed him a sideways coquettish glance. 'Oh yes indeed, sir, I will look forward to it.'

Dorothy thought to herself that it was high time Suzanna was safely married and away from Kirklee Castle. She would have to arrange for that to happen as soon as possible. She began to wonder about the dancing assembly at the Saracen's Head. Perhaps matching Suzanna and the honoured guest there would be a possibility, an outcome that could only enhance the standing of the family.

CHAPTER SEVENTEEN

They used sedan chairs for the journey from the ladies' flat to the Saracen's Head Inn. The sedans were carried into the dark wynd leading to the main street by trotting Highlanders preceded by a man holding a torch aloft to light their way.

Eventually reaching the inn, they climbed the outside staircase clutching at their skirts, then made a lively splash of colour as they crowded into the lobby together. Dorothy rustled in striped silk in shades of pink and greeny-grey. Suzanna blossomed in an open gown of apple green which showed off her embroidered petticoat. Lord Lamond was resplendent in a scarlet coat and white breeches. They swept from the lobby directly into the dancing room.

Soon Dorothy and Lord Lamond were dancing a stately minuet but Dorothy declined to join in any of the wild Scottish dances. It was not in her nature to behave with such abandon. Suzanna, on the other hand, flung herself joyously into the spirit of the dances and was whisked away time after time by both Lord Lamond and the young Duke of Skye.

Scottish people, Dorothy realised, were still very strange to her. There was a tartness about so many of the women's tongues, a dour perverseness about a surprising number of the men, and a hidden passion about all of them. This passion could unexpectedly burst out at dancing assemblies among the most respectable and even elderly ladies. They bounced to their feet and with astonishing energy, whisked about the room, every now and again screeching like polecats.

Suzanna was becoming overexcited, Dorothy felt. Surely this would not give a good impression to the Duke. It was imperative that he saw her behave in a more ladylike and restrained fashion. She tried to catch Suzanna's attention to warn her with a disapproving look, all to no avail. Suzanna's behaviour was most disturbing. She was racing and whirling about the room, almost in tears with laughter.

Eventually Dorothy did catch her attention and signalled to her that she wanted to speak to her. Suzanna came staggering and gasping with hilarity.

'Sit down,' Dorothy commanded. 'To allow yourself to become so uncontrolled is unladylike, especially in a hooped skirt.'

'But Dorothy, everybody...'

'Sit down, Suzanna!'

Suzanna, recognising the icy note in her sister's voice, knew better than to challenge it. Still laughing and choking for breath, she sat down. Dorothy shut her fan with a click.

'In France, people go to a dancing assembly to meet other people. In Scotland, they come for nothing but the dancing. An assembly room is like a field of exercise – very uncouth exercise for the most part.'

'But so very enjoyable,' Suzanna said. 'And I do like the noble Duke, don't you?'

The gentleman in question sauntered over

just then and with a little bow and a smile, he asked, 'Have you had enough, Suzanna?' Dorothy replied before Suzanna had the chance, 'I'm afraid she has, sir. It is high time that we returned to our apartment, and to bed.'

Lord Lamond joined them. 'Nonsense,' he said, 'we have not yet had supper. And it is time now. See, everyone is beginning to make their way upstairs.'

The assembly room had stopped its mad whirling and screeching.

'Oh very well,' Dorothy said, and rose to follow the others.

She flapped her fan energetically to help clear the stench of sweat and perfume that hung heavy in the air and mixed with the smoky candles. When they reached the place where they were to have supper, Suzanna sat on one side of the Duke and she sat on his other side.

They were all getting on splendidly, talking and laughing at some of the Duke's adventures abroad and hardly giving a glance to the food that was placed before them, far less noticing any of the serving wenches, until suddenly Dorothy saw Isla.

'Well, well,' Dorothy said to Alice Raeburn who had also made a beeline for the noble duke and was sitting nearby. 'Do you recognise one of the servants, Mrs Raeburn?'

Mrs Raeburn looked around. 'It's not...?'

she began.

'Indeed it is,' Dorothy said. Then when Mr Menzies came over to see if everything was to their liking, Dorothy said to him, 'Well sir, I have no complaints about the food, but your servants – or at least one of them – is definitely not to my liking.'

Mr Menzies looked taken aback.

'Has one of the wenches offended you, your Ladyship?'

'Indeed she has, sir. She had offended me greatly with her impertinent tongue.' She indicated Isla who was now near enough to hear her.

'Isla Anderson, you mean?' Mr Menzies queried.

'I'm surprised, Mr Menzies, that you saw fit to employ such a wild creature in your respectable establishment. There's no telling what she might do or say, or how she might offend any of your other customers. I fear I must warn the lords and ladies of my acquaintance.'

'No, no, your Ladyship, there's no need. I will tell her to return to the kitchen immediately and to stay there.'

At that point, Isla came nearer to Lady Lamond and the proprietor, hips swinging, a haughty lift to her head, an impertinent gleam in her eyes. 'Your Ladyship,' she addressed Lady Lamond, 'it is my pleasure to serve you with some of this delicious trifle.

133

It is the Saracen's Head speciality.'

Before Dorothy could say anything, Isla had flung the bowl of trifle into Lady Lamond's face. There was silence in the room as everyone gaped in astonishment and horror at the apparition of Lady Lamond – her face, her hair, her beautiful gown – all dripping with a mixture of cream, cake, almonds, jam, jelly, wine, cinnamon and froth. For a few seconds, the only sound in the room was of Lady Lamond spluttering and choking.

The Duke of Skye was the first to recover. 'Get that mad woman away from here,' he ordered Mr Menzies.

'Yes sir, I'm sorry sir.' Mr Menzies grabbed Isla and dragged her roughly away.

The Duke shouted after him.

'Call the guard. Have her flung in the Tolbooth jail.'

'Yes sir, yes sir,' Mr Menzies called out in distraction. He daren't look round to witness yet again the dreadful state of Lady Lamond. 'This could ruin me,' he hissed at Isla, 'ruin the good reputation of my inn.'

'It's not your inn,' Isla flung back at him. 'It belongs to the ugly old harridan of a wife you married.'

Mr Menzies struck Isla a blow across the head. 'I'll have you whipped through the streets,' he told her, 'and the streets is where you'll stay. No-one – no-one, do you hear me – will ever give you a place again. By

God, I regret the day I did! Obviously I was completely taken in by you, you lying little harlot.'

Isla had reeled for a few seconds under the impact of his blow but quickly recovering herself, she swung her knee up into the man's groin causing him to double up and clutch at himself in agony. Taking advantage of the freedom from his grip, Isla dashed along the lobby and out of the building.

It wasn't until she was flying along the dark street that she remembered about her bag containing all her possessions. Now she only had what she stood up in. Even then, she had to strip off and discard the Saracen's Head apron and cap in case it might help the guard to identify her.

Darkness and despair, thick as thieves, closed in all around her.

CHAPTER EIGHTEEN

Even after she returned to Kirklee, Lady Lamond had still been upset by the dreadful experience she had suffered at the Saracen's Head, and she had taken to her bed to recover from the shock. Meanwhile, Esther was not the only one at Kirklee who had laughed to herself and blessed Isla Anderson when she had heard about it.

She would be the talk of the town. That would be what was really bothering her, Esther thought. The humiliation of it at the hands of a serving wench!

Hiding her true feelings, Esther forced herself to be most solicitous, offering her Ladyship a calming potion which helped her. Far from being grateful, however, Lady Lamond had treated her even more like a servant, ordering her to do this, to do that. 'Put the potion there just now and make up more so that I can keep a bottle in my store cupboard. I will not have you fussing about like a woman in her dotage, disturbing me with your inane chatter.'

Only Lord Lamond thanked her for helping his lady. Poor Lord Lamond. He deserved better than the cruel, heartless shrew he had got for a wife. She was not even beautiful with her hard watchful eyes and small tight mouth. What did she care about him or about anyone? Isla was not the only person to have been dismissed. Poor Effie and Annie had been sent packing in floods of tears, and it didn't bear thinking about where they would end up. Now even Cook and Mrs McGregor were sick with worry about their own positions. Both were no longer young and Kirklee had been their home for most of their lives.

As the days dragged by, Esther became

more and more certain of one thing. Lady Lamond had to be stopped. Lord Lamond had remarked one day, when Esther enquired about her Ladyship's health, that she was not sleeping so well as she used to. 'But,' he assured her, 'your herbal potion has helped, Miss Nichol.' (He still called her Miss Nichol, never 'Nurse' – a sign of respect for which she was most grateful.) 'Her Ladyship couldn't do without it.'

If only there was no Lady Lamond, what a different life they would all have. What peace. What security. What happiness. She owed it to everyone, not only to herself, to rid the place of the woman. Yet each time she thought of actually putting her longings and her thoughts into action, she felt horrified at herself. She went down on her knees in the privacy of her tiny shabby bedroom and prayed for forgiveness and the strength to resist her dark thoughts.

But she had no strength. She had never been a strong woman, either in body, mind or spirit, and her thoughts became ever darker. Two problems began to constantly fill her mind. Firstly, if she did ever administer the poison to Lady Lamond, how could she avoid harming anyone else? Secondly, and this terrified her, what would happen if she was found out?

She became obsessed with thoughts of poisoning and the terror of what the consequences might be to herself. It made her unable to concentrate on anything or anybody else. Finally, having taken Theresa out for a walk, and resting for a time by the river, she had returned, incredibly, without the child. So obsessed, so distracted was she with her thoughts, she had forgotten the child. She was appalled at what she'd done and was running back in great agitation, not even caring when her cap fell off and her lank hair was revealed tumbling down over her shoulders, when Lady Lamond stopped her.

'Have you taken complete leave of your senses? Why on earth are you running about like a mad woman?'

She'd had to confess and Lady Lamond had been coldly furious. She had ordered her to come to the drawing room after she'd returned the child safely to the nursery.

Esther knew then that she had no choice. She could not allow Lady Lamond to dismiss her. Fortunately Lord Lamond was away in Edinburgh. He was not due back until the next day. Nobody need know about the dismissal which Esther knew was about to be meted out to her, as indeed it was and in the most insulting and humiliating manner. In a cold fury, Lady Lamond had ordered her to pack her bags and be out of the house at first light the next day. If she was not gone by then, her Ladyship would have her thrown off the premises.

Later that evening, Esther hovered about the kitchen, awaiting her opportunity. She discovered that one of the maids had been instructed by Lady Lamond to bring her an extra strong hot toddy that night to take along with the herbal potion.

In anticipation of this fateful day, Esther had already used all her expertise to prepare a special poison and now, clutching a tiny phial of this lethal concoction, she watched the movements of the maid. It was quite easy really. The girl put the whisky into a pewter tankard with the honey and while she went over to the tap to fill the kettle with water, Esther put a few drops from her phial into the tankard without anyone noticing. The girl boiled the kettle on the fire, filled the tankard with steaming water, gave it a brisk stir and left the kitchen carrying it on a small round tray. Esther had calculated that the amount she had administered to the drink would take a few hours to do its work. Daylight should see the end of Lady Lamond.

As Esther expected, there was a terrible stir in the house in the middle of the night. Esther lay in her bed wide awake and listening. Feet pattered about on the stairs, voices were raised in distress. Eventually there was a knock on her bedroom door. She arose and wrapped a robe around herself.

'What is it? Who is there?' she called out.

'Oh Miss Nichol, it's Janet,' the maid cried

out. 'The mistress has taken poorly. Miss Suzanna has sent for the doctor but meantime she asks for you to come and see if you can help the poor lady.'

'Tell her I will be there as soon as I can,' Esther said.

Quickly she dressed and then made her way swiftly towards Lady Lamond's bedroom. There were several maids – as well as Suzanna – in attendance, all crowding helplessly around the bed. Lady Lamond was thrashing about, her eyes protruding and wild in a scarlet face. Suzanna was trembling with agitation.

'Miss Nichol,' she greeted Esther, 'what can be wrong with my poor sister?'

Esther sighed. 'She has taken a fit.'

'Is there anything you can do? God knows when the doctor will arrive.'

Esther bent over the writhing figure. She imagined she saw recognition and hatred in the wild eyes for a moment. Esther felt panic-stricken. Maybe yet again the woman would get the better of her. Lady Lamond's mouth, bleeding now, was struggling to form words. Her hands were clutching at Esther's dress. Horrible animal grunts mixed with the now incessant weeping of the maids. As Esther leant close to the tortured face to mop her brow, Dorothy stared straight into her eyes and uttered one last word. In a barely perceptible whisper, Esther, and only

Esther heard her say,

'*Murderer!*'

Then suddenly Lady Lamond's body stilled. She lay there almost peaceful now. Except for the terrible look of anguish on her face.

Esther gently closed Lady Lamond's unseeing eyes, straightened, beginning to breathe more easily, thankfully. With all the weeping and wailing that filled the room she was sure no-one could have heard. Or understood. She looked round at Suzanna.

'I'm afraid she has gone.'

'Gone?' Suzanna's bewilderment increased. 'Why, what do you mean?'

'Lady Lamond is dead.'

Suzanna began to weep along with the maids. Esther took charge and shooed the maids out.

'Go down to the kitchen and make some tea.' Esther turned back to Suzanna who was now sobbing helplessly into her hands.

'I don't understand. What can be the cause of this?'

Esther sighed. 'The truth is – and I hate to tell you because your sister wanted to spare you and his Lordship the knowledge of it – she has been suffering several small seizures over these past months. I have been trying to help her and I wanted her to consult the doctor as well, but she would not. She didn't want to make a fuss. You know how she never liked fuss and she did not want to worry or distress you or Lord Lamond. But I feared, right from the beginning – indeed I knew – that these seizures could get worse and the result could be, alas, as we see now.'

'How could I or Lord Lamond not have known?'

'They happened mostly when you and his Lordship were out having a day's hunting or a few days away at Glasgow or Edinburgh.'

'Oh, poor Dorothy,' Suzanna wailed. 'Poor Dorothy. God rest her soul.'

'God rest her soul,' Esther echoed piously.

CHAPTER NINETEEN

It was late, and the taverns were spewing out their drunken occupants. Isla had been crouched for hours, it seemed, in one of the dark stinking closes in the Trongate. At least there she was sheltered from the blustery wind and needles of rain that were gusting down the street.

It had been as silent as the grave for a long time, but now the Trongate and beyond burst into riotous sound. Coaches drew up, sedan chairs arrived, horses gathered outside every tavern. The heartiness and thoroughness which characterised the prosperous Glasgow citizens in their business and commercial pursuits was equalled in their social life. They enjoyed everything with boisterous high spirits, not least their food and the pleasures of the table. In the taverns that night they had feasted on rounds of beef, roasted sirloin, mutton boiled and roasted, Scotch haggis and cock-a-leekie soup.

Now gentlemen who had lingered over the flowing bowl were being escorted, supported, sometimes carried out in varying degrees of unconsciousness, by their servants. Those who had not collapsed into complete oblivion were enjoying a loud and tuneless sing-song, the whole scene bathed in the flickering amber light of carriage lamps, as the men leading the sedan chairs held their lanterns aloft to help guide the servants.

Isla stood up and pressed her body against the wall of the close. Although no-one could have seen her in the blackness. Gradually, the sounds died away. The flickering lights were swallowed up by the night and the Trongate fell silent once more.

Isla began to shiver again. She ventured out onto the street, but in a few minutes was soaked to the skin and colder than ever. Reluctantly she returned to the close, unable to see any other option but to spend another night there. She couldn't sleep, not only because of the bitter cold and discomfort, but from the fear of the dark shadowy figures that began to gather around her.

Nobody spoke. She could see by the dawn's grey mist seeping through the close that they were beggars. Some hunched down on the stairs, others sprawled out on the ground. Isla cringed back from the sour stench of the rags that they wore. Once it was light enough to see her way properly, she clambered over the sprawl of bodies and out onto the street, stiff and sore and miserable, as well as tense with the need to empty her bladder.

She didn't know where to go or what way to turn and eventually she wandered up the Candleriggs. There she slipped into one of the black closes to relieve herself before continuing towards the Back Cowloan. She wept with shame at the state she was now reduced to, with her creased, soiled clothing, her tangled mess of hair and filthy face and hands.

The thought of spending even more nights in such misery was too painful, and she banished it from her mind. It occurred to her that she had only one alternative now and that was to make for The Glasgow Bell, the hostelry that belonged to her stepfather. Remembering her stepfather's groping hands, she knew only too well the difficulties and dangers she would face there too, but face them she must. In any case, despite her current sorry state, she still believed she was

144

more than a match for any man – her despicable stepfather included. And so, apprehensive but resigned to the fact that anything was better than the misery of the previous night, she set off for the hostelry, which was situated a couple of miles beyond the Back Cowloan, across fields and up hilly paths.

Soon she could see hordes of navvies busy digging an extension to the canal which already stretched from beyond Kirkintilloch. She remembered how the canal had been a favourite topic of conversation between the Lamonds and their friends. Many of the ladies (with the exception of Mrs Raeburn) had urged their husbands to oppose the canal building. But Lord Lamond, no doubt influenced by his friend David Hudson, argued that it would be good for commerce. Already many influential Glasgow merchants had added shares in the Forth and Clyde navigation to their interests in West Indian trade and cotton importing.

There had been disagreements among gentlemen too, but they were mostly based on east-west rivalry. When one Glasgow gentleman had asked, 'What is commerce to the city of Edinburgh, sir?', the gentleman from the east had replied, 'Edinburgh, sir, is the metropolis of this ancient kingdom, the seat of law, the vender of politeness, the abode of trade, and the winter quarters of all our nobility which cannot afford to live in

London; for these and other reasons equally cogent, Edinburgh ought to have the lead upon all occasions. The fools of the West must wait for the Wise Men of the East.'

Nevertheless, according to Lord Lamond, a dynamic Glasgow group were well on their way to taking complete control of the canal. They included the wealthy merchants whose skill and ambition had promoted Glasgow's trade throughout the world.

Isla kept as clear as she could of the canal workings. She had heard many wild tales about the navvies and did not feel capable at that particular moment of coping with any trouble they might cause her.

Eventually, footsore and weary, The Glasgow Bell came into view. A two-storeyed whitewashed building, its roof half-thatched and half-slated with crow-stepped gables at either end, it stood close to the bank of a recently completed part of the canal. At the back there was a large cobbled yard and stables to accommodate many horses, coaches too. Isla wondered what sort of job her stepfather had made of the hostelry since she had last set eyes on it. At least there would be a decent roof over her head, a comfortable bed to sleep in and a good fire to warm her. She could deal with her stepfather. She wasn't a child any more and he would now find her a force to be reckoned with.

As she came nearer to the building, she

was taken aback by the loud noises that were issuing from it. There were alarming crashes and rough voices raised in anger. She stood at the door, shaken by the coarse and obscene language she could hear from within. Eventually mustering all her courage and determination, she opened the door and went in.

CHAPTER TWENTY

Esther wore her best dress for the funeral. It was a grand affair, although Esther was quite sure that the villagers and estate workers who turned out did so as a mark of respect to Lord Lamond, not to the late Lady Lamond. But there they all were, lining the road, heads bowed, men with hats clutched in their work-roughened hands, their wives and daughters with their heads respectfully covered.

Esther had taken charge and organised the funeral meal of roast mutton and boiled potatoes followed by a steamed pudding, all washed down by a plentiful supply of claret. Immediately after Lady Lamond's death she had discarded her nurse's apron and cap and had now resumed her rightful place in the house as a kinswoman, one of the family.

She had also arranged for Mrs Ritchie, a widow woman from one of the cottages on the estate, to take over as nurse for Theresa.

It was a raw autumn day with a bitter wind that tugged at their clothing and brought rain that chilled the mourners to the bone. Everyone was glad to get back indoors after the burial and enjoy the hot brandy possets that Esther had instructed the cook to prepare. Afterwards they savoured the meal which had been supervised by Esther to make sure that everything was perfect.

This was her happy day, and her happiness was complete when not only Lord Lamond, but Hamish Raeburn, complimented her on how well she had organised everything. Suzanna never said thank you. She was too busy giving the Duke of Skye an alarming time with her sobbing and swooning into his arms. As a result, he was planning to take her home with him so that, as he said, she could rest and recover in the beautiful and peaceful surroundings of the island of Skye.

That, Esther felt sure, would be the last they'd see of Suzanna. From the first moment Suzanna had met the Duke, she'd obviously set her sights on becoming the Duchess. Esther hoped that she would succeed. In her opinion, Suzanna was too vain and flirtatious for her own good. Nevertheless, she wished the girl no harm.

Hamish Raeburn had also been grateful to

her for yet again bringing relief to his distressing symptoms. He had found her valerian and meadowsweet most soothing and relaxing. Not only had it given relief to his head pains, but he had noticed a distinct improvement in the digestive upsets that he was also a martyr to.

A few days after the funeral they met while out riding and she had sat him down on a boulder while she stood beside him and administered healing to his head and neck. He had been grateful almost to the point of tears for the relief and comfort she had given him and before they went their separate ways, he had reverently bent over her hands and kissed them.

Later she had received a formal letter of thanks from him which had begun, Dear Miss Nichol. She had replied with equal formality but had suggested, for his continued benefit, another meeting.

That meeting had been equally successful. Indeed he had written in glowing terms to tell her so. She had replied with a letter which had daringly begun, *My dear Mr Raeburn*, and in which she had admitted that she too found comfort and pleasure in their meetings.

After the next time, during which they had enjoyed a pleasant stroll together, while he had gone into some detail about his latest symptoms, she had given him the potion that she had prepared for him. She had not been going to perform the laying on of hands that day because their walk had taken longer than they first realised, so happily had the time flown past. However, he pleaded with her with such earnestness that she complied. How could she refuse the poor man? He looked so pathetic and indeed in need of attention in many ways. Even his clothes looked as if they had just been thrown on. She would dearly have liked to reprimand his rascal of a valet.

When she had done her healing, she could not resist the impulse to tidy his hair and fuss at his neck cloth and tug and tweak at his coat until he looked passably smart and presentable. He went on his way very con-tented and happy, or at least as contented and happy as any man could be who was married to such an uncaring woman as Alice Raeburn.

His next letter began, *My dearest Miss Nichol*, and had affected her deeply. His gratitude and his sincere appreciation of her talents had always been expressed in his letters, but now there was a dependency and an attachment to her that was extremely touching. Poor man, she kept thinking. He should never have got himself tied to that woman. She is no use whatsoever. He needs someone like me at his side all the time to care for him and to look after him.

She told him as much in her next letter and his quill had responded immediately with a fervent, *Oh, my dear, if only such a heavenly situation could come to pass. Oh, what a happy and deeply honoured man I would be.*

He had repeated this again at their next meeting. It had set her thinking.

Then suddenly her happy euphoria was shattered. Alice Raeburn appeared at Kirklee and demanded to see Lord Lamond alone. Lord Lamond had turned to her and smiled.

'Do you mind, Esther?'

She had been sitting doing her embroidery and thinking about Hamish Raeburn. She looked round in surprise. Alice Raeburn was on her own, a most unusual occurrence. She always visited in the company of her husband.

Esther rose in somewhat of a flutter. She hovered outside the door in an effort to hear what was being said. The thick studded door, however, was soundproof. Reluctantly, and more than a little apprehensive, Esther went downstairs and through to the lower drawing room. Unable to settle there, she went to the front entrance and opened the door. The Raeburn coach stood outside, the horses impatiently pawing the ground. Then there was the clicking of shoes on the stone stairs and Alice Raeburn swept into view, her enormous hooped dress filling the stairway. She passed Esther with only a disdainful glance and was helped into the carriage by a footman before it clattered away down the tree-lined drive.

Esther stood for a few minutes watching it disappear into the distance.

'Miss Nichol.'

She turned to the maid who had just called her name. 'Yes, Janet. What is it?'

'The master wants to see you in the upper drawing room.'

'Very well.' Esther retraced her steps up the stairs and into the drawing room. Lord Lamond was lounging back in his chair. He looked slightly amused.

'Well, well, Esther. I am surprised. You are the last person I would have thought to be accused of scandalous behaviour.'

Esther's cheeks tingled with heat.

'Scandalous behaviour, my Lord?'

'Surely you cannot deny it. I have seen the letters.'

'If you are referring to the correspondence between myself and Mr Raeburn, I can assure you, Lord Lamond, it was perfectly innocent. I have a high regard for the gentleman and we are good friends. There is nothing scandalous about it, I do assure you.'

'I'm afraid I disagree, my dear, and Mrs Raeburn is much distressed, as well as angry. I really do think it would be better if you left Kirklee.'

'Left, my Lord?' Esther stared at him in bewilderment.

He shrugged. 'For a time, at least. Perhaps Mrs Raeburn will calm down and forgive your foolish behaviour eventually. Perhaps if some distance is put between you and Mr Raeburn, you will recover from your foolish obsession with him.'

Esther made a valiant effort to control her trembling.

'But my Lord, I do assure you...'

'Now, now,' Lamond interrupted, 'Mrs Raeburn knows, Mr Raeburn knows, I know, and even you must realise, Esther, that it is more than friendship. It is best for everyone concerned that you should go.'

'But ... but ... where can I go, my Lord? This is my home.'

'I will arrange that you will stay in Glasgow with my aunts for the time being.'

'In *Glasgow?*' Esther echoed in shocked disbelief.

'I will send a letter to the ladies explaining the situation. Now you'd better go and start to organise your packing.'

In a daze, Esther turned away and slowly left the room.

CHAPTER TWENTY-ONE

There had been such a drunken riot going on that no-one had noticed Isla standing inside the doorway. She raced towards the stairs and, taking them two at a time, reached the top in a matter of seconds, grabbed a lighted candle from the table in the lobby and dashed into the nearest bedroom, locking the door behind her.

She was horrified at the change in The Glasgow Bell. It had been such a quiet and respectable place when she'd lived here with her mother. She could feel the floor throbbing under her feet with the fighting and thumping and noise that was going on downstairs. There were sounds also of breaking glass. The customers were obviously ransacking the place. Why wasn't her stepfather doing anything to stop them, she wondered. This state of affairs couldn't be allowed to continue. If things carried on like this, she might as well be back out on the streets.

In the morning, once everyone had left, she would tackle her stepfather and ask him what on earth he was thinking of to allow such behaviour under his own roof. Meantime she was exhausted and needed to get a few hours sleep. She held the candle over the bed, bare of everything except a sagging mattress. She opened a cupboard and discovered some blankets. They looked clean enough and she hauled them out and used them to cover herself as she lay wide-eyed and stiff-limbed on the bed. She remembered how quiet the place had once been. The customers had been a few local farmers, or travellers on their way to Glasgow. Her mother, with the help of an elderly woman called Mrs Fraser, had kept the place clean and cooked good, wholesome food. It didn't seem as if there was anyone helping now and the people frequenting the hostelry must be the navvies working on the canal.

She'd heard Irish and English voices, Highland too, as well as local accents. At first there had been only local men working on the canals. Gradually, Highlanders had appeared. Then the English arrived and even a few Irishmen as well. Clusters of huts had sprouted all over the countryside. The canal that was being built was eventually supposed to connect Edinburgh with Glasgow, and she could understand how it would quicken the pace of travelling and ease the transportation of goods. It was, in fact, already doing so.

But the building of it was causing a terrible upheaval in the countryside. The making of a canal, it seemed, involved much more than the task of digging. As well as navvies, there were groups of craftsmen like masons, joiners, brickmakers, and blacksmiths. Quarries were being opened for free stone, limestone and rubble. Kilns had been built and roads had been made. Cranes had been erected and reservoirs constructed to regulate the flow of water and the leading of feeders of streams to the canal. Often this was by way of aqueducts and tunnels. All this was what the opponents of the canal never stopped saying was an ugly gash on the landscape. But nothing shook the enthusiasm of the Glasgow men when it came to commercial enterprise and profit.

Even they, however, were not so enthusiastic about the navvies. Lord Lamond had spoken to one of the engineers, a man, he said, of gentlemanly and retiring nature, whose dealings with the rough navvies were distressing him greatly. Indeed it seemed, Lord Lamond remarked, that he was mightily terrified of them. Remembering this remark brought defiance surging through Isla's veins. She'd be damned if she'd allow a crowd of noisy ruffians to terrify her!

With that she turned on her side, shut her eyes and composed herself to sleep. Soon all noise had faded, leaving only a still silence.

Isla was awakened by the early morning light filling the room, revealing layers of grey dust and the depressing shabbiness of the place. She swung her legs from the bed, sat up and listened intently. There was no sound of a broom sweeping up the debris, no clatter of pots from the kitchen. She left the room and went cautiously down the rickety timber steps.

As she came into the long bar room, the nauseating stench of urine, vomit and tobacco filled her nostrils. Carefully, her face twisted with disgust, she picked her way through pools of congealed sick and up-turned tankards, as the wan sunlight filtered in through the dirty bottle-glass windows.

The floor, part earth, part flagstone, was littered with bottles, dirty pewter plates, and broken glass. The circular iron wheel that held the candles hung askew from the smoke-blackened ceiling. The candles had not been snuffed out but some had guttered low and wisps of black smoke instead of flame were drifting from them.

Sprawled across the top of the bar counter lay the unconscious form of her stepfather. She made her way over to him for a closer look. He stank of whisky. Retracing her steps, she went out of the back door and into the yard. There she filled a wooden bucket with cold water from the well, before return-ing with it and flinging the contents over her stepfather's head. He came to with a splutter and a howl as he struggled to his feet.

'Eh, who's that? Wha's that?' he mumbled

incoherently, peering at Isla with bloodshot eyes.

'It's Isla, Archie.'

'Isla? Isla?' he echoed.

'Your stepdaughter. I've come home to stay. I've come to help you.'

He stared at her in silence for a moment, and then to her horror and astonishment, he began to cry. Tears poured down his face, his shoulders shook. He wiped the snot from his nose with the back of his sleeve.

'Stop your blubbering,' Isla said. 'What's the meaning of all this? You're allowing customers to wreck the place.'

'Wait a minute, hen,' he said, staggering over to the shelves and clutching at a bottle of whisky. 'I can't think or do anything until I've had a drink first.' With that, he tipped the bottle to his mouth and took several deep swigs of it.

'Oh, I see,' Isla said. 'I see what the problem is now. You're drinking so much you don't know what you're doing or what's happening.'

'I'll be all right now that you're here, hen. You were always a spunky wee lassie. A bit on the wild side, mind. But what in God's name brings you back to this...' And there he paused for a moment, surveying the chaos around him. Taking another swig from the bottle, he continued 'to this fine hostelry? I mind the last time I saw you, and the sound flogging I got for my trouble!'

'Never mind that now,' said Isla, 'I think it will be for the best if we both let bygones be bygones. All you need to know for now is that I'm going to save you and The Glasgow Bell from ruin.'

'If ye can do that, lassie, you're more than welcome here. God knows I've tried, but since the canal came the place just hasn't been the same. You'd never believe half the things those navvies get up to.'

'Oh yes I would!' Isla replied, 'I've already seen more than enough to know what they're capable of, and if I've anything to do with it they'll not be carrying on like that much longer.'

A broad smile creased Archie's crimson, weather-beaten face. 'Where have ye been all these years lassie? Hell, this place would've been mighty different if ye'd no run away like that.'

'As I said, that's all in the past. From today, we both start afresh. Like it or not, you and I and The Glasgow Bell are going up in the world.'

'I'll drink to that!' said Archie, raising the half-empty whisky bottle in a grubby hand. And despite squalor of the scene, Isla couldn't help thinking back to the day the Earl had rescued her outside this very inn. Her luck had changed that day, and perhaps now it was changing once more.

CHAPTER TWENTY-TWO

Back and forth, back and forth Isla trudged from the well in the yard to the bar-room with buckets of water to throw across the flagstoned part of the floor. The earthen part proved more difficult but after several attacks with rake, wire brush and shovel, she managed to clean it up too. She scrubbed the bar and the shelves, she wiped bottles, she washed pewter plates and tankards.

Archie was pathetically grateful. 'What a transformation,' he told her. 'By God, you're a great wee worker, hen.'

'Oh, shut up. Just leave off the drink,' Isla told him impatiently. 'Your job's not to let this ever happen again. You were letting that crowd ruin the place.'

'Och, the lads are workin' hard out there. They need a wee refreshment at the end of their day's work.'

'A wee refreshment,' Isla cried out incredulously. 'Don't be ridiculous. Anyway, it doesn't matter how little or how much they drink, they don't need to make such a filthy mess. They're like a crowd of animals. We're going to lay down a few rules from now on.'

'That's all very well for you to say things like that, hen, but what can I do? I mean, they're no' goin' to pay any attention to me. I tried. Honestly, I did try.'

'Well you didn't try hard enough and by God, they better pay attention to me. And it's high time you put down that bottle, Archie. The first thing is you'll need to be sober to deal with them.'

Archie sighed. 'It's no' much of a life if I cannae get a wee drink.'

'A wee drink! You drink non-stop by the looks of things.' Isla wiped at her brow with the skirt of her dress. She was hot and breathless and sweaty with her hours of hard work.

'Just try and sober up,' she told Archie. 'I'm going out to get a breath of fresh air.'

There was a bit of paving at the front of the building and a couple of rustic seats. Then there was a grassy bank and a towpath running alongside the newly dug canal. The water had a dark sparkle in the wintry sunshine. Isla took a few deep breaths and savoured the cool air on her face and bare arms and feet.

At this particular stretch of the canal, all was quiet and still. But further along, towards Glasgow, she could see navvies with their cranes, tackles, piling engines and pumps. The sun glinted on the metal of their spades as sods flew from them into the air.

She leaned back against the door lintel, suddenly realising how exhausted she was. Soon darkness would settle over the canal and the countryside, and the navvies would lay down their spades and come crowding in to the hostelry again.

Isla closed her eyes. She had been right to come here. Despite all the hard work that lay ahead. By sheer good fortune she now had a chance to make something of herself. The Glasgow Bell might be on the verge of ruin, but the sad state it was reduced to had given Isla her opportunity. If The Bell had been successful and Archie a prosperous and able landlord he would probably have thrown her back onto the street. But she had the upper hand now. He was a weak and pathetic drunkard. She was young and determined. In no time at all, she promised herself, she would be mistress of a thriving hostelry, able to hold her head high in any company.

As she stood there in the dark in her half-sleeping state, she could hear the barrows and handcarts being wheeled along temporary boardwalks, the hard bumpy sound echoing through the still air. She gave herself a little shake and forced herself to return indoors.

Through in the back kitchen, she found Archie tossing potatoes into a huge black iron pot.

'Is this what you give them?' Isla asked.

'Aye, they're great ones for the tatties, especially the Irishmen.'

'What kind of meat do you serve with them?'

Archie gave a mirthless laugh. 'I don't serve them at all. I just put the pot out and they all dive in. I used to have meat when there was Jeannie Fleming here to cook it, but she soon left like the rest of them.'

Isla shook her head. 'What a shambles! No wonder there's no quality ever come here now.' She found a big jug and sat it in a basin, then filled the jug with the hot water from the kettle.

'I'm away up to my room to have a wash and see if that'll waken me up. I'm absolutely exhausted. That had better be the last time that I've to face all that mess. I didn't come here to be a slave after you or any other man.'

She trudged up the stairs carrying the heavy basin and jug then deposited it on the small marble-topped table in the bedroom. Archie, she had discovered, had one of the other rooms at the end of the corridor, the same room that he had once shared with her mother.

When her mother had been alive, the place had been kept spotlessly clean and tidy. She remembered the pristine white bedspread, the gleaming wood floor, the glass case above the fireplace in which Archie had kept his brace of pistols, the rosewood chest of drawers, the piers glass, the round table so highly polished you could see your face in it. Isla daren't think what an unholy mess there might be in that room now. She determined that once she got the place properly organised, she would get a girl from Glasgow to come and help to keep the place clean.

She poured some of the hot water into the basin and washed her face and hands. Far from refreshing her and wakening her up, however, the hot water only made her more sleepy. She decided to flop down on the bed for a moment or two's rest. She must have fallen almost immediately into a deep sleep because the next thing she knew, the room was in darkness and there were riotous sounds issuing from downstairs.

Damnation, she thought. Archie had allowed them to go berserk again. It was too much, especially after all her hard work cleaning the place and getting it in order. She jumped from the bed, hurried from the room and downstairs to the kitchen. There she picked up a heavy black cast-iron skillet and rushed forward into the wall of sound.

She was confronted by a scene from Dante's *Inferno*. Heavy smoke coiled and swirled in the soupy atmosphere. The acrid smell of male sweat burned her nostrils. Over at one side of the long room, a ring of men were yelling encouragement to four battling navvies in the centre of the circle.

Without stopping to think, Isla rushed forward and using the edge of the pan, she slashed viciously across the knees of the first two protagonists. They dropped to the stone-flagged floor screaming curses. The younger of the two remaining backed off to howls of derision from the watching pack. The remaining navvy licked his lips and clenching and unclenching his ham-like paws, shuffled forward. Isla swung the skillet with both hands in a furious upward, back-hand swing, crashing the pan across the cheek of her opponent. His eyes rolled upwards and he dropped unconscious to the floor.

The crowd were now roaring with drunken hilarity. 'What a little beauty,' someone called out.

Isla experienced a surge of panic as the ring of red, beery faces turned on her. She felt the heat of the crush of bodies closing in her. Wildly she tried to swing the iron skillet around but she was grabbed from behind and then somebody caught hold of her hand and wrenched the weapon from her. She felt real terror now. Although she kicked and screamed and lashed out with every ounce of her strength, it was no use. Coarse hands were already on her breasts and tugging up her dress.

Then suddenly she heard a shout that

reverberated throughout the room and cut through the racket of the men.

'That's enough! The next man who touches the girl will be out of a job tomorrow.' The voice acted like magic. A sulky silence replaced the bedlam. The men slunk back, leaving Isla shaking so much she had to hold on to a chair to prevent herself from collapsing.

Through the haze of smoke in the room, she saw David Hudson emerge and come towards her. He was a giant of a man, the tallest man she had ever seen, with enormous shoulders and muscly thighs straining in tight breeches. There was an excessive maleness about him. She had sensed it from the first time she'd met him. She could see it now in his black, knowledgeable eyes. She could smell it from him.

'I'm surprised to find you in a place like this, Isla,' he said, a note of genuine concern in his voice. 'Lord Lamond told me you'd left Kirklee, but I didn't realise you had fallen on such hard times.'

Ignoring his remark, Isla said haughtily, 'If these are your men, Mr Hudson, you should be ashamed of yourself. They may be able to dig very well but they certainly don't know how to behave.'

Hudson picked up the skillet and handed it to her. 'Perhaps the same could apply to you and I suggest after this, you keep to your place in the kitchen and use this for what it was meant to be used for. That way no harm will be done.'

Bloody cheek, she thought furiously. Before she could think of a reply to put him in his place, she caught sight of Archie Anderson slinking in behind the bar from wherever he had been hiding.

Her fury turned on him. 'Bloody coward,' she shouted at him. 'You've always been the same. Lifting your fist to women and children is the only thing you've ever been any good at.'

Archie shook his head and smiled apologetically towards Hudson. 'She's an awful lassie, this. You never can tell what she's goin' to do or say next.'

'What's she to you?' Hudson asked as if Isla wasn't there.

'My stepdaughter, sir. I never could do anything with her.'

'Ha, you're right there,' Isla shouted derisively, 'and what's more, you're useless with anybody or anything.'

With that, she stormed out of the bar and went through to the kitchen. She was shaking with fury now and when Archie eventually followed her, she said to him,

'I've only been here a couple of days and already I'm sick of the place and everything about it, especially you.'

'Oh, wait a minute, hen. You're surely no'

thinking of leaving again? You could be the making of the place.' His voice was filled with the desperation of one who knew his last chance was slipping through his fingers. Somewhere deep down he knew she would be the saving of him and The Bell. He had to make her stay. Whatever the cost.

'We could be partners, eventually, you and I. I could get it all drawn up legal. God knows, I've no-one else to leave the place to when I'm gone, and you're the nearest thing I have to a real daughter. And after the shameful way I treated your poor mother, it's the least I can do. We could make a real good thing of it between us if we just put our minds to it.'

Despite herself, Isla was moved by Archie's honest admission of his past guilt. But she wasn't about to let him see that. 'We? Between us? Our minds to it?' She sneered. 'A lot of good you'd be as a partner or anything else!'

'All right, all right,' Archie said. 'We could make it that you'd have the most say in it. You could run it whatever way you liked as long as I get enough out of it to live on and have a wee bit refreshment now and again, I'd be quite happy. And after my day, it would all be yours. Think about it, hen. It would be like having your own place and as I say, you'd be the boss.'

Isla hesitated. The truth was she had had

no intention of leaving. She was not going to be beaten by a crowd of ignorant savages.

'I'd want to make sure it was legal. Where would we go to get that done?'

Archie said, 'Edinburgh. We'd have to go and see old Mr McTaggart. He was a lawyer friend of my father's and he lives and works in Edinburgh now.'

'All right, first thing tomorrow morning we're off to Glasgow to get the first stage-coach from the Saracen's Head.'

Archie had not thought she'd want to move so quickly. He began to have second thoughts about what now seemed to be an over-generous offer.

'But how could we leave here, hen? I mean somebody's got to be here to see to things.'

Isla, however, was determined to hold him to his word. If she didn't, there was no telling what might happen if he sobered up, or changed his mind or – God forbid! – returned to his old bullying ways.

'You're not going to wriggle out of this. It's got to be done legal or not at all. We can lock and bar the place and put a notice up outside saying when we'll be back to open it again and we'll need to start early as I said, so we'll need a few hours rest. You'd better go through and get rid of all them and lock up for the night.'

'Oh, it's no' so easy to do that, hen. I mean, they just don't pay any attention.

They leave in their own time.'

'Oh, for goodness sake,' Isla said pushing past him, 'have I to do everything myself?'

Through in the bar-room she was surprised to find it silent and deserted. She was thankful too, and went over to the door, turned the key and shot the bolt.

CHAPTER TWENTY-THREE

A man kept talking to her. He was an elegant looking young gentleman sitting opposite her in the coach. He had pointed out places of interest to her during the journey, and at first this had passed the time well enough. Archie meanwhile was hunched in a corner, sound asleep. Also crushed into the coach were three other men, all looking as old and dull as Archie Anderson.

The young gentleman, Isla had learned, was called Henry Forbes-Mathieson. Now he flicked a hand towards the scene outside the coach window and said, 'This is the backbone of Edinburgh.'

'It is a mighty bumpy one,' Isla remarked.

They were all being heaved and jolted this way and that as the coach wheels struggled up the roughly cobbled street.

'And one could say,' Forbes-Mathieson

went on, 'that from this backbone all the narrow wynds and closes jutting out on either side are the ribs.'

Isla said, 'It looks a fascinating place.' It was a long narrow street and according to Forbes-Mathieson, was called the Royal Mile. It was lined with overhanging buildings from which a multitude of flapping garments were hanging out to dry on poles protruding from windows. There were dark entries which gave glimpses of tortuous obscurities, some leading down steep, narrow passageways. The road itself was a crush of coaches and carts and a dangerous jostle of sedan chairs. One sedan came so close, its occupant – a perky madam with a loop of amber beads swinging from her wig, wearing a low cut gown and wielding a flirtatious fan – peered into the carriage to admire unashamedly Henry Forbes-Mathieson. He was admittedly looking very elegant in a high-coloured coat of russet red velvet and a waistcoat of white silk with gold embroidery in a delicate floral design. Forbes-Mathieson, however, was too taken up with Isla to even notice the woman. He didn't look a bit tired, despite the fact that he had been happily talking non-stop throughout the journey.

But Isla was no longer favourably impressed, either with his appearance or his conversation. His tiresome observations and rather brittle charm had in the end only added to the fatigue of the long and uncomfortable journey. Now they had finally arrived every street seemed steep, treacherous and crowded and their horses' hooves clattered and slithered most alarmingly.

At another time, the town might have seemed romantic to Isla with its palace on the flat ground at one end rising in an increasing crush and jumble of towers and rooftops to a mighty castle at the other. However, on this occasion, she was only intent on practical matters. As far as she was concerned, the quicker the legal business was completed and she was back putting The Glasgow Bell to rights, the better.

Henry Forbes-Mathieson was now asking if she would have tea with him as soon as they arrived at the inn. Isla politely declined, explaining that she and her stepfather had to seek out without any delay their lawyer, a Mr McTaggart, with whom they had important and urgent business.

'Supper then,' the gentleman insisted.

'We'll see, we'll see. It depends how long our business takes,' Isla said, somewhat impatiently.

Just then Archie, who had been dozing for most of the journey, woke up with a start. 'Is this us? Are we here?'

'Just about,' Isla replied.

Sure enough, within a couple of minutes,

the coachman was reining back the horses and the coach had come to a halt. Isla felt stiff with sitting for so long. Nevertheless, she was impatient with the way Henry Forbes-Mathieson fussed over helping her from the coach. 'I can manage,' she said and swished away past him into the inn. Despite her fatigue, she would have been ready to venture out again immediately after they had been shown to their rooms and deposited their cloak bags. Archie, however, pleaded for a few minutes so that he could have a drink.

'I'm parched,' he said, 'and we'll have to get another coach. Mr McTaggart's place is away at the other end of Edinburgh and it's getting dark already.'

'All the more reason that we set off as quickly as possible,' she told him. But by this time, Archie had ordered his dram, thankfully gulped it down, and ordered another. Eventually Isla had a pot of tea and was glad of it because it revived her body and spirits.

Then, not listening to any more of Archie's pleas, she dragged him from the bar and into a carriage that would take them to Mr McTaggart's place of business.

The carriage hadn't gone very far when a dense fog suddenly descended. The coachman said it would be as difficult to turn back as to go on. He lit the carriage lamps which burned dimly and ineffectually, shedding precious little light on their gloomy surroundings.

'Oh, do hurry,' Isla called out to him impatiently.

'I'm sorry, miss,' he replied. 'It's impossible to move any faster.' The horses in fact were stepping very gingerly along, as were the people on foot in the streets, who were mere shadows now, feeling their way beside walls, windows and doors and bumping into one another. To Isla, there was something eerie about such a vast city wrapped in this oppressive darkness with lamps burning in the streets and torches flashing weakly on peering faces.

Isla held a handkerchief to her mouth and tried not to cough. It was as if all the smoke that had ever gone up from Edinburgh's chimneys had been kept somewhere above the clouds to rot, descending now, thick and foul-smelling, to catch at the throat and make the chest wheeze.

At long last they reached the lofty building in which Mr McTaggart had his legal practice. Isla and Archie made their way, shuffling carefully, towards the dimly lit entrance. Even inside the building, there was a clammy haziness.

During the negotiations in Mr McTaggart's high-ceilinged and gloomy room, Archie tried at first to water down the proposals he had originally agreed with her. However, Isla did not allow him an inch. As far as she was concerned, it was all or nothing at all. At least that is what she insisted to both Archie and Mr McTaggart.

In the face of Isla's persistence Archie soon wilted, consoling himself that he would probably have lost The Bell soon enough anyway if things didn't change. Now, at least, if Isla made The Bell a success once more, he would share in that success.

When the formalities were over, McTaggart poured them all a glass of port to toast their new partnership. 'To The Glasgow Bell,' said McTaggart, and with a clink of glasses, the deed was done.

On their return to the inn where they had booked in to stay overnight, Archie made straight for the bar, while Isla ended up having supper with Henry Forbes-Mathieson. She would have preferred to be on her own but he insisted on joining her. Finally she escaped, pleading fatigue. After all, as she pointed out to him, he could sleep late into the next day whereas she had to be up at the crack of dawn to leave with the stagecoach to Glasgow.

It was when they were out on the street early next morning awaiting the readiness of the coach that Archie was hailed by a giant of a man, built like a pugilist, with a grotesque distorted nose.

'Mr Anderson,' the man called, 'what are you doing through in Edinburgh.'

'Oh, hello there, Jake,' Archie said, 'I could ask the same of you.'

'I've been at my mother-in-law's funeral.'

Now that the man was closer to them, Isla could see that his nose wasn't broken, it was partly decayed – eaten away into holes. For a moment, Isla had to avert her eyes.

'What are you working at these days?' Archie asked. 'And what on earth's happened to your face?'

The man sighed. 'Och, I'm a chrome-worker in yon chemical works. It's a hellish kind of place, and ye ken that chrome has a terrible effect. Naebody lasts long at it. I'm sure it'll be the death o' me yet.'

'Why do you no' try and get a different job then?' Archie said.

Jake shrugged. 'Don't think I havnae tried, but I'm no fit enough for the canal now, and what else is there aroond here? And I cannae risk leaving unless I've somewhere to go. I've a wife to think about.'

As one whose own fortunes had only just taken a turn for the better, Isla could not help feeling sympathy for Archie's friend. She had an idea. 'Look,' she said, 'we're needing help to run The Glasgow Bell. How about if you came to serve at the bar and help us keep a bit of order in the place? Your wife would be welcome too. She could keep the place clean and maybe do a bit of cooking. We couldn't afford to pay much in the way of wages at the moment, but we could give you a decent roof over your head, plenty of food in your belly and enough ale to drink.'

The man's eyes widened, his disfigured face quivered with incredulity. Isla thought for an embarrassing moment that he was going to drop to his knees with gratitude.

'Oh, mistress,' he said, 'Ah cannae thank ye enough! Wait till I tell the wife, she'll no believe it! It's the answer to all our prayers.'

'Hey, wait a minute,' Archie piped up. 'What do you mean – plenty of food in their bellies and enough ale to drink?'

'Remember what we agreed,' Isla said. 'What I say goes and I say we need help and Jake, I'm sure, is just the man for the job.'

'Oh aye, mistress, oh aye, you can be sure of that. Me and the wife will work like slaves for you – and gladly.'

'All right, that's it settled then. Archie, put your hand in your pocket and give Jake enough to pay for him and his wife's journey on the next stagecoach to Glasgow.'

Afterwards Archie grumbled and whined his objections during most of their return journey to Glasgow. Eventually Isla told him to shut up in no uncertain terms. She believed she had done the right thing. It would be well worth the few coins that Archie had so reluctantly parted with, to have someone as solid and loyal as Jake about the place the next time she had to deal with a mob of drunken navvies.

CHAPTER TWENTY-FOUR

The journey from Edinburgh had been a tiring and dusty one. Isla felt badly in need of a good wash. The inn was closed until the next day and so the place was quiet and deserted. Jake and his wife had not yet arrived, and Archie, as usual, was stretched out in his room, dead to the world in a drunken stupor.

Isla went out to the yard armed with a bar of soap and a large towel. She stripped off and began splashing herself with the cold water, soaping her body and then splashing it again. She danced about as she did so, shivering at the same time with the icy tingle on her skin.

It was while she was doing this that she heard to her horror a deep male laugh. She swung round clutching the towel against herself. There, lounging against the stable wall across the yard, was David Hudson. Even from this distance, she could see the dark glimmer and feel the animal magnetism of his eyes.

Isla was furious as well as acutely embarrassed. 'How dare you?' she shouted at him. 'How dare you stand there and watch me?'

He shrugged. 'It's a hostelry, is it not?

'The front door's locked and there's a notice stuck up on it saying that the bar isn't open until tomorrow.'

She tugged the towel around her as best she could.

'I didn't wish the use of the bar at this particular moment,' he said, 'only the watering and the stabling of my horse.'

Still clutching at the towel, Isla turned and forced herself to walk nonchalantly towards the back door and into the building. She wanted to run as fast as she could, she was so angry and embarrassed, but she didn't want to give him the satisfaction of thinking he'd had any effect on her at all.

Once safely upstairs in her bedroom, she clenched her fists and banged them against the wall. She felt like banging her head as well, she was so angry. From the first moment she'd met him, he had infuriated her. But she had also felt she'd come up against someone stronger than herself and not just in the obvious physical sense. She felt a hardness and an immovability about him very like the wall that her fists were now pounding against. She struggled for control. She was being ridiculous, she told herself.

What did it matter what David Hudson was like? He had nothing to do with her, or her life. She began vigorously rubbing herself dry with the towel and after dressing, she went downstairs, forcing her mind onto matters of business.

There were four rooms downstairs as well as the long bar-room. She had been thinking of setting up one of them for the use of gentlemen who wanted to gamble, having seen how Lord Lamond and so many of his gentlemen friends indulged in this expensive pastime. With this in mind she strolled around the room thinking about how she could improve it, make it comfortable and inviting enough to attract men of the right sort. Men like Lord Lamond.

As soon as Jake and his wife arrived, she would get them started on cleaning up the room. Then she would get Archie to furnish and equip the room to the required standard. Once it was ready, she would send a notice to Lord Lamond inviting him to come with his gentlemen friends to enjoy an evening's gambling. It wasn't the first time she'd sent him a communication. She had written a letter of condolence after the death of his wife, at the same time apologising profusely for the regrettable incident at The Saracen's Head. Isla had not expected a reply, considering how scandalous her behaviour on that occasion must have seemed to Lord

Lamond, but a few weeks later she received a letter from Kirklee. In it, Lamond graciously accepted her apologies, writing,

'It is not in my nature to be vengeful. What is done is done. It is in the past and I intend to let the matter rest, particularly in view of recent tragic events.' At first Isla thought he was referring to the death of his wife, but as she read on she discovered to her horror that the old Earl had also died. Hearing of Dorothy's demise, he had decided to leave Rome and return to Kirklee. But his ship had foundered in a terrible storm as it neared the Scottish coast. All on board had perished. Isla wept bitterly as she read this awful news, but vowed to herself that, as long as she lived, she would never forget the old Earl.

Lamond ended his letter by wishing her well in her new life, and suggesting that he might call in at The Glasgow Bell, as he was often in Glasgow attending to matters relating to his investment in the canal.

Before any invitation went out, however, Isla would have to make sure that the barroom was properly regulated. There must be no more rioting and brawling. She would welcome the navvies' custom and give them good service as well, as long as they behaved in a reasonable manner.

That night, Jake and his wife, Molly, arrived. Molly was a small timid woman with saucer eyes and dry wisps of hair escaping from the white linen cap that fastened under her chin.

Isla showed them up to the attic where there was a large area, cam-ceiled but with good proportions, and with some odd bits and pieces of dusty furniture lying around, including bed ends and a bedspring. A row of small windows looked out onto the canal.

'Do you think you could do something with this place for yourselves?' Isla asked.

'Oh, aye, aye,' Jake said. 'Sure we could, Molly?'

Molly vigorously nodded her head.

'Oh thanks, missus, this is awful good of you. We'll make this into a wee palace, so we will.'

'Come back down with me just now to the kitchen and we'll have something to eat,' Isla said, 'and I'll give you some pillows and blankets for the bed.'

It was agreed that first of all Jake and Molly would put the attics to rights. After that, and from then on, they would be working downstairs. And so it was that the next morning, they were up early to assist the workmen Archie had hired to equip the gambling room with its new fixtures and fittings. By the end of the day Isla was amazed at the transformation. The once seedy and run-down room was now resplendent, with freshly painted walls in a tasteful crimson hue, a polished teak floor, sparkling gilt candelabra and candlesticks, red velvet chairs and a chaise longue of the highest quality, a pair of enormous ornate silver-gilt mirrors, and, at the centre of it all, a magnificent mahogany gaming table with green leather insets, finished off with exquisite gilt tooling. Isla was sure her gambling room would not have disgraced the Saracen's Head – or even the mighty Tontine Hotel for that matter.

A few days later everything was complete, all that the gambling room needed now was the right sort of patrons. Isla sent Jake on horseback to deliver the notice and invitation to Lord Lamond, then she waited in suspense and some anxiety to see what the response might be. Most of her anxiety was to do with the navvies when they came for their usual drinking session in the main bar room after work on the canal finished for the day. She was determined that they would not be allowed to spoil her chances of attracting regular gentleman customers. It was these gentlemen who would be the making of The Glasgow Bell, perhaps not on the first night they came – if indeed they did come. But once the gambling room was established, Isla saw herself making a great deal of money from their patronage.

Jake returned having left the message, but he brought with him no reply. They would just have to wait.

Meantime, the navvies rolled noisily in. They immediately started thumping on the bar and bawling out their orders. The crowd that came in next immediately fought their way forward. With a sinking feeling, Isla watched as the usual chaos developed. The evening had hardly started and already there was bedlam. God forbid, if any gentlemen arrived in the middle of this disgraceful carry-on! All her hopes for the gambling room would come to nothing.

Isla knew she had to act quickly. She raced upstairs, along the top corridor and into Archie's bedroom. There she tugged open the glass case above the mantelpiece and took out his pistols. She loaded them as she'd seen him load them in the past. Then she rushed downstairs again, clambered up onto the nearest end of the bar counter, and discharged one of the pistols into the ceiling with an ear-splitting crash. The crowd of navvies immediately fell silent, partly from shock, and partly awed by the magnificent sight of Isla, wreathed in gunpowder smoke and covered in dust from the fallen plaster, aiming the second pistol directly at them.

'Any of you bastards want a bullet in your belly?' She yelled into the shocked silence, 'Well now's the time! Otherwise drink your ale and behave like men, not animals. If you do that tonight and every night – do you hear me – every night from now on, we'll get on just fine. Otherwise there'll be hell to pay – and don't worry, I'll be keeping these pistols handy!'

There was an uncertain, hostile murmur from the crowded bar, but before it could grow into genuine defiance, Isla called out again, 'You think I wouldn't shoot? Try me!'

Suddenly one of the men called out, 'By God, I believe you would, hen. You're a right spunky wee lassie, aren't you?'

At that the crowd broke into jovial laughter, and another shouted out, 'Maybe we should send her tae sort oot thae damned Frenchies and their wee revolution! She'd soon have 'em all behavin' themsels!' His comrades let out a great cheer, and huge peals of laughter filled the room. In that moment the danger was passed and Isla knew she had won an important battle. She had won their respect – no easy thing with men as hard-bitten as these.

'Just enjoy your ale and a talk and a laugh, that's all I ask.' Isla shouted over the din, before climbing down from the bar.

She turned to Jake. 'Jake, pile some more logs on that fire. We want a nice cheery blaze for the men's comfort and warmth. Then smarten yourself up – and you too, Archie – and serve our good customers. We don't want to keep them waiting.'

Taking her place behind the bar counter Isla put the pistols on a shelf underneath it.

'Right now, gentlemen, who's next?'

There was laughter all around. 'Oh, now we're gentlemen, are we?' somebody said.

'You behave like one and I'll treat you like one,' Isla countered. It was then she noticed Hudson in the background. She didn't know whether he had been there all the time or had just entered the room, but he was standing with his thumbs hooked in his belt, grinning over at her. She'd never known a man who could infuriate her so much, and most of the time without even saying a word. Indeed, at that moment she might have succumbed to a mad impulse to shoot him, had she not heard the tinkling of the bell she'd left in the gambling room.

She rushed immediately along the down-stairs corridor. In her notice she had suggested that gentlemen would find it convenient, after stabling their horses, to enter by the door in the yard. From there, they would find the first door on the right to be the entrance to the gambling room. Now, when she entered it, half a dozen gentlemen – including Lord Lamond – were already settled round the table. A cheerful log fire was burning brightly in the hearth, and candles flickered all around.

'Good evening, my Lord, I hope you enjoy your game. There is no time limit – you are welcome at this table the whole night long if you have a mind to it. Now, is it to be claret, or port, or ale? Just tell me your pleasure.'

'Congratulations, my dear Isla,' Lord Lamond said. 'I was somewhat concerned about how you might fare, but it seems I had no need to worry.'

'You had no need to trouble yourself, my Lord, I have always been able to look after myself. And may I say how honoured I am that you have deemed The Glasgow Bell worthy of your custom. I trust you will not be disappointed.'

He smiled at her. 'From what I have seen so far my dear Isla, this cosy little retreat from the cares of the world will more than suffice. Now, fetch the claret, and we shall all enjoy our game.'

She smiled at him in return. What a very handsome and charming man he was. He had no need to be so kind and considerate. He could take his pick of any of the finest establishments in Glasgow. But he had chosen to come to The Bell, and when word spread that he was a customer, other men of quality would follow his lead. Isla was sure that Lord Lamond would realise this, and she could not help wondering why he should bestow such good fortune on her.

CHAPTER TWENTY-FIVE

Isla was getting to know the navvies. There was Seamus who could play the fiddle, filling the bar room with merriment and laughter with his jigs and reels. He was a long leek of an Irishman who couldn't seem to get clothes to fit him. A naked strip of leg always showed in the space between his trousers and his boots, while the sleeves of his shirt never reached his knobbly wrists. His face was long and cadaverous, yet he had the brightest, liveliest eyes that Isla had ever seen. At least when he was playing the fiddle. He really came to life as soon as he gripped the instrument under his chin, twirling merrily about, his feet noisily tapping in time with the music.

Sometimes Isla gave him free drink if he'd been playing for most of the evening. Sometimes he played well-known songs and the men joined in with lusty roars. Isla had worried about the noise of their singing, in case it annoyed the gentlemen along the corridor in the gambling room. But when she had asked them they had assured her that it was of no account. Nothing, it seemed, could divert them from the pleasures of their game.

In any case, by the time any singing began, the gentlemen were often as inebriated as the navvies.

The navvies themselves got so drunk sometimes that they got up to face each other, not in a fight but in a dance. Flinging their jackets to the floor, they would cavort about to the sound of the fiddle in shirt sleeves and waistcoats, heavy-booted feet clumping back and forth, their hats or bonnets jammed on the back of their heads.

Eddie was quite a nimble dancer who could lift his knees higher than anyone else and always looked a colourful sight in his green shirt and red neckerchief and his hat always at a jaunty angle. The men laughed uproariously at Eddie's dancing acrobatics but they clapped encouragement to him as well.

Big Harry was more of a worry to Isla. He was a good-natured lump of a man but easily persuaded into a fist fight for a wager. She'd forbidden any fighting in the bar room, only to discover that a fight had been arranged out in the yard at the back. There had been a terrible noise of shouting and she'd rushed out to find not only navvies, but gentlemen, congregated in a howling mob yelling encouragement to one or the other of the bare-knuckle fighters on whom they'd bet large sums of money. Big Harry was one of the fighters.

Afterwards, Isla had dragged him into the

kitchen where she'd washed his wounds and told him what a fool he was to allow himself to be battered about like that. Already he'd had his nose broken twice and his face was permanently discoloured and marked from the punishment he'd taken. She had forbidden any more fights to be conducted in the yard but knew that they would just move into one of the fields nearby instead.

'I worry about you,' she told Big Harry. 'I don't like to see you hurt like this.'

Big Harry had given a joyous laugh. He had a laugh as loud as a foghorn.

'Fancy you worrying about the likes of me!' He was absolutely delighted. 'You're a great wee lassie, so you are. It's worth getting battered in a fight just to hear you say that.'

Isla groaned and gave up. The best she could do was tend to him when he staggered back to her in The Bell after each fight, like a giant puppy dog eager to be patted.

'You're far too good to that man,' Old Ben, one of the other navvies told her. 'He's no' right in the head. I don't know why you waste your time and trouble with him.'

Old Ben was one of the quieter navvies who never got drunk and just sat quietly in a corner smoking his pipe and enjoying a leisurely pint of ale. He was the oldest of all the men working on the canal and he'd once confided in Isla that he'd lost his wife and his two children to the smallpox. They'd had a nice wee house in Glasgow but since he lost his family, he couldn't bear to set foot in it. He couldn't face being anywhere on his own. The company of the men and the hard toil along the canal went some way to prevent him thinking about his loss.

'These lads aren't a bad crowd once you get to know them. A bit rough and ready maybe, but after what they put up with on the canal they need to take their ease and sup their fill. The work's harder than any other I've known.'

Isla agreed that the men weren't so bad once you got to know them and that included Old Ben himself. He was a kindly man and she'd been very touched when one day he'd presented her with a string of amber beads that had once belonged to his wife.

'My wife was a servant in a big house before we married and the mistress, a good woman who'd been fond of my Mary, gave her the beads for a wedding present.'

At first Isla had refused the gift which Old Ben had obviously treasured but he'd insisted.

'What use are they to me? You're a bonnie lassie and you've been that good to all of us here. I'd like you to have them. You'll make an old man happy if you'll take them. I know that you'll treasure them as my Mary did.'

191

Isla had given him an affectionate kiss and promised that indeed she would treasure them.

She had helped Molly to make a big pot of mutton broth to serve to the men every night to help keep their strength up. It was worth the extra work to see how the navvies relished the steaming soup. Word had got around and navvies were coming from miles away to enjoy the food and drink and homely atmosphere of The Glasgow Bell.

One person who was enthusiastically spreading the word despite a terrible disability was a young lad called Charlie who had a dreadful stutter. He had no family except his fellow navvies who were normally patient with him but had begun teasing him about his obvious devotion to Isla. He was a freckly-faced young man with a thick mop of red curls. He would do anything for Isla and was always struggling with much contortion of mouth and face muscles to ask if she needed any help.

'C ... c ... c ... a ... a ... a ... nn I ... I ... hi ... hi ... hi ... elp you, I ... I .. Isla?' he would plead as he followed her about.

She sometimes allowed him to carry a heavy tray for her. Or occasionally the jug of washing water up to her bedroom. He was much teased by the other navvies about this.

Charlie found that if he sang words he didn't stutter them, and he took to singing to her everywhere she went. Not only the men found this habit hilarious, but Isla was hard put to it not to laugh at Charlie herself. Not wanting to hurt his feelings, however, she managed to keep a straight face and listen in all seriousness to his unusual conversation.

David Hudson was often to be found in the company of the gentlemen in the gambling room. More and more, however, he was coming into the bar room and having a drink there as well. Sometimes he spoke to the men. Sometimes he sat by himself. Isla became aware of his dark eyes continuously watching her. His unwavering stare made her feel uncomfortable and resentful. As far as she was concerned, he spoiled the relaxed friendly atmosphere of the place. She couldn't fathom why a charming gentleman like Lord Lamond was so friendly with such a man. They had nothing in common – except the canal, and their love of gambling.

Each time she became aware of Hudson staring at her, she felt sure he was remembering how he'd seen her naked that time in the yard and she flushed with embarrassment and anger.

Sometimes he smiled at her and his smile was like a secret caress. It fuelled her anger and made her long to throw a pint of ale in his face. She refused however to give him the satisfaction of seeing that he could upset her.

She concentrated all her attention on the navvies, flirting with them and sometimes even joining in their singing and dancing.

In comparison, she was always very sedate and dignified when she went through to attend to the gentlemen's needs in the gambling room. There she blossomed under Lord Lamond's admiring gaze and generous compliments.

Isla had begun to suspect that she was falling in love with the noble Lord. Although the very notion was ridiculous, the idea excited her. In the privacy of her upstairs bedroom she could ignore the harsh reality of the situation and allow her mind to fill with wonderful dreams of an impossible romance.

CHAPTER TWENTY-SIX

With each day that passed, Isla's happiness increased. Things were working out even better than she'd hoped. Admittedly the navvies were as boisterous and noisy as ever, but they were good-natured with it now and so she didn't mind. There was a happy atmosphere about the place, and the reputation of The Bell as an excellent hostelry had spread far and wide.

The main thing that was exciting her though was the success of the gambling room. It was never empty. Isla had even opened up the adjoining room and furnished it to the same standard to accommodate these extra customers. Gentlemen, many of them Lord Lamond's aristocratic friends, were attracted by the welcome they received from the beautiful hostess, not to mention the good food and drink they enjoyed, served by the two pretty serving wenches that Isla now employed.

For the most part Isla supervised everything now rather than serving, but she was always there to give a friendly welcome to the gentlemen and show a lively interest in them and their affairs. Three of the rooms upstairs had been made ready for travellers needing overnight accommodation, and one of the rooms downstairs, the one nearest to the kitchen, had been converted into a dining area where a hearty breakfast of bacon and eggs, sausages, black pudding, potato cakes, butter, cheese and fresh sourdough bread, baked on the premises, could be served to the guests.

Molly had sent for her young sister Helen to come and help and part of the roomy attic area had been made into a room for her and the other two serving wenches.

Isla wasn't being quite so successful in keeping Archie Anderson from drinking too much. It was difficult when drink was so easily available. Even so, she was making some progress. At least he didn't drink himself unconscious every night.

There was one other turn of events that she hadn't originally planned on. Lord Lamond had begun to show a romantic interest in her. Oh, she had had her dreams and she certainly had a fancy for him, but she had never really believed that her admiration and affection would be reciprocated. Why would a member of the aristocracy want her when he could take his pick of any of the finest ladies in the land? Then she would examine herself, her reflection, in her piers glass. She would look at her long auburn hair, her clear skin, her bright green eyes and think, Why not? She had enough good looks to please any man and she dressed and behaved like a lady. Nowadays, she welcomed her guests resplendent in silks and satin, dresses every bit as good as the ones that the old Earl had given her. Her particular favourite was a beautiful creation in apple green silk, low-necked and wide-skirted, with lace flounces at the elbows. Dressed in such a way as this she retained her pert self-assurance in the company of any man, including Lord Lamond, but she couldn't help revealing some of her excitement to Molly.

'Imagine, Molly,' she said in a whisper so

that none of the others in the kitchen could hear her, 'he has invited me to have tea in the castle and is sending his carriage for me tomorrow. I'm so excited. Truly I am.'

Despite her attempt at discretion, however, Archie had overheard. He grinned. 'She'll be mistress of that castle yet, Molly. Just you wait and see! I wouldn't put anything past my Isla.'

'I'm not your Isla,' she said. 'And why shouldn't I end up lady of Kirklee? I'm every bit as good as any lady that's ever lived there.'

'I know, hen, I know,' Archie agreed, obviously delighted with the whole idea.

'The only thing is,' Molly ventured, 'what about Mr Hudson?'

Isla was genuinely surprised.

'What about him?'

'You must have noticed, Isla. He never takes his eyes off you when he's here, and he's here every day now.'

'Oh, he watches me, I know.' Isla flicked a dismissive hand. 'He's just that kind of man. I can't abide him.'

She was aware of course that all the men watched her. She didn't mind their admiring glances for the most part but Hudson's dark penetrating stare was different. That was what annoyed her so much about him. If she was completely honest with herself, he frightened her too. She'd rather die than show that fear, of course. She'd fought against Archie and she'd fight against Hudson too, if the need arose. But although, thanks to the old Earl, she had escaped from Archie all those years ago, echoes of that fear she had felt, that sexual threat, still remained. Not as far as Archie was concerned any more. He was a feeble shadow of the man he had once been. She could fell him with one blow now, she felt sure, if he ever was stupid enough to try anything again. But he wasn't that stupid. He knew which side his bread was buttered on. She had transformed The Glasgow Bell and they were making a very good living from it.

She wasn't nearly so sure about Hudson or how he might behave given half a chance. So far, she hadn't give him any chance at all, just in case.

'Och well,' Molly said. 'I don't know why you've taken such an aversion to the man. He seems a nice enough fellow to me. Good-looking chap too.'

'He's nothing but a rough navvy,' Isla said, secretly feeling guilty about talking so disloyally about men who were now not only her good customers, but her good friends.

'He's not a navvy,' Archie said. 'He's a contractor. From what I've heard he owns most of the canal. He's got shares in it. Just the same though, he's nothing compared with a lord in a castle!'

Isla laughed.

'Lord Lamond has only asked me to the castle to enjoy a dish of tea. He hasn't asked me to marry him.'

'Oh, but if you play your cards right, hen, I'm sure that's what it'll come to. His Lordship is obviously very taken with you. And since his wife died they say he's been awful lonely up there, and his poor wee daughter without a mother...'

'Nonsense,' she scoffed, but secretly she was pleased. She had come to believe that Lord Lamond was indeed enamoured with her. She had even started to dream fantastic dreams of becoming his wife and living again in Kirklee Castle. Oh, how sweet that would be! She'd invite the family to the wedding of course. The dowager Countess, Miss Esther Nichol, the two ladies. She would make the servants all dance a pretty dance as well. She had not forgotten how they had once treated her. Oh, how they would have to change their tune! It would be – your Ladyship, yes, your Ladyship. They would have to curtsey to her too. Just to imagine it made her smile with happiness.

Then there was that awful woman Alice Raeburn and her pathetic husband. Isla remembered how Hamish Raeburn had kept making cow's eyes at Esther Nichol. She wondered what had become of them. She didn't think Hamish Raeburn would have had enough courage to do any more than give adoring glances, but Miss Nichol was a different story altogether. Although she looked like a timid little soul, Isla had always suspected that there was no telling what she might be capable of.

CHAPTER TWENTY-SEVEN

Miss Nichol had never lived in a tenement before and she suffered agonies of bruised pride every time she climbed up or down the stairs of the building in which the ladies had their abode. Every inch of the dark, evil-smelling close, each grubby, littered stair, every part of the damp walls was a torment to her, cried out to her– 'Look at the depths to which you have sunk. This hell on earth will be the death of you.'

She had been afraid to write to Hamish Raeburn and plead for his help in case the letter fell into Alice Raeburn's hands. She had in fact received a letter from him advising her not to take this risk. In his letter he assured her of his deep concern – more – his undying affection for her. He missed her. He missed their walks, their talks. He confessed that in his tender years he had been dominated and completely cowed by his mother and now in his maturity, it was the same with his wife.

It had been such a joy for him to meet a gentle person like herself who had treated him with such sincere affection and respect. From his childhood he had, in the name of discipline, been treated by his mother most cruelly until she had completely broken his spirit. He remembered his home as a kind of prison where he was whipped daily and locked in a cupboard where he sobbingly repeated Latin verbs until he could recite them with a perfection that was never quite perfect enough for his mother. He was usually given yet another whipping and sentenced to bread and water.

Why had he been so foolish as to marry such a woman as Alice Raeburn? She was the replica of his mother in build and looks, but with her own particular brand of cruelty.

'I cannot tell you, Miss Nichol,' he wrote, 'why I allowed myself to be caught up in her snare. Oh, how many times I have wept in secret and regretted my foolishness. How many times have I wished that I had met you sooner in my miserable life. We could have been so happy together. Now I have not even the pleasure of your company as a friend to bring some light and solace to my sufferings.'

Then one day when she was walking along

the Trongate to deliver material to the ladies' mantua maker – joy of joys – she unexpectedly bumped into her dear Mr Raeburn.

They went into the Tontine for a dish of tea and a long heart to heart talk from which both drew great comfort. Daringly, before they parted company, he took her hands in his and kissed them most tenderly. They arranged another meeting and it was only thoughts of that tryst that sustained Esther Nichol as she completed her errand for the ladies and then returned up the tenement stairs.

Already the stair was crowded with stinking vagrants and beggars and the snugness of the flat in which she now lived with the ladies did nothing to alleviate the horrors of what lay outside their door.

The ladies had both been suffering from a cold and a chest cough. Esther, who'd brought with her her medicine chest, and a good supply of herbs and potions, had offered to help them. At first they had preferred to send for their doctor, a decent and serious-minded man of whom they were very fond. His medicine however had such a putrid taste that it made the ladies sick. They were forced in the end to try Esther's herbal cure which had been mixed with whisky and suited them very well.

Esther had read much of the Edinburgh Pharmacopoeia, the doctor's bible, and was not surprised that so many of the recipes in it tasted so vile. The ingredients included things like the juice of wood lice, pigeon's blood, spiders' webs, powder of human skulls, shavings of elk's hooves, frogspawn, human blood, fat and urine, and excrement of horse, pig, peacock and goat.

After they'd all had supper she excused herself and retired early to her bedroom. There she sat on the rocking chair, rocking her small frame gently backwards and forwards by the fire and thinking about her love. She imagined how wonderful it would be if they could be together as man and wife. That is how it ought to be. They were meant for each other. She had never been so certain of anything in her life. It occurred to her, as she sat staring sightlessly into the fire, that this beautiful, happy state could come true. She could make it come true. It was quite easy really. All she needed to do was give Hamish Raeburn the same potion to give to his wife as she'd given to Lady Lamond.

She had the means to free him of his misery. She could show him how he could change his life. Change both of their lives. Quietly she retrieved her medicine kist from underneath the bed, began mixing the fatal potion, then carefully poured it into a glass phial.

She could hardly wait for her next meeting with Mr Raeburn. She sang about the flat that morning but quietly, under her breath, so that the ladies would not hear her singing and remark on it. Then the time came at last, and she hurried to meet her first and only love. They sat close together in the Tontine again and after initial greetings and pleasantries, Esther asked,

'Do you genuinely wish to be free of your domineering wife, Mr Raeburn?'

'Indeed, indeed, Miss Nichol. Oh, if only I could do something, anything, to be free of her. I pray every day for something, anything, to happen to free me from her. What a joy, what a relief, a blessed relief it would be if my prayers were answered.'

'My dear Mr Raeburn, your prayers have been answered.'

Esther's face was aglow with eagerness and happiness. Mr Raeburn was taken aback.

'I do not understand, Miss Nichol,' he said in some bewilderment. 'My wife was as much married to me as she ever was when I left her in her drawing room no more than two hours ago.'

'Let me explain.' Esther took the phial from her glove bag. 'In this phial is your freedom, Mr Raeburn. I've heard Mrs Raeburn say that she likes a hot toddy at night. All you need to do is pour the contents of this phial into her glass and by morning, she will be gone. You will be a widower, Mr Raeburn, with everybody lavishing every sympathy, kindness and support on you.'

Mr Raeburn had gone a sickly grey and he was staring at the phial like a transfixed rabbit.

'Here, take it.' Esther Nichol pushed it towards him. 'It will be so easy, I do assure you. There is nothing to worry about.'

Mr Raeburn's head began to shake uncontrollably.

'Oh... I... Oh ... no ... I... Oh, Miss Nichol. No, it is unthinkable. It is much too dangerous. I am not a brave man, I admit it. I can't help worrying. I am a worrier, Miss Nichol. What if something went wrong, I ask myself.'

'Nothing will go wrong, Mr Raeburn. Please believe me.'

Mr Raeburn looked near to tears of distress.

'But how can you know, Miss Nichol. How can you be so certain? Nothing in life is certain.'

'Death is certain, Mr Raeburn. I watched Lady Lamond die of this potion. That is how I know that it works.'

'You ... you ... mean you, you mean...?'

Mr Raeburn's voice faded into silence. Eventually he was able to speak.

'I am sorry, Miss Nichol, but I feel quite faint. You will have to excuse me. My delicate constitution, you know. I will recover shortly. Meantime I must not risk embarrassing you by drawing attention to my plight in a public place.'

'Of course,' Miss Nichol replied in anxious sympathy. 'You are considerate and thoughtful as ever, Mr Raeburn. Is there anything I can do to help?'

'No.' He hurriedly rose, clattering the table back as he did so. 'I just need to get out to the air, then return as quickly as possible to my bedchamber to rest. Forgive me, Miss Nichol.'

And before Esther could even say goodbye, he was gone.

CHAPTER TWENTY-EIGHT

David Hudson had taken to coming in for breakfast every morning and then going through to the bar for a tankard of ale. Isla, who had dressed very early in eager anticipation of the carriage that was to take her to Kirklee, had draped her velvet cloak over a chair and was standing warming herself at the bar-room fire when Hudson came through.

'Going to Glasgow today are you?'

Before Isla could answer, Archie, who had been polishing the top of the bar counter, piped up,

'Not a bit of it, not a bit. She's been invited to go up to Kirklee Castle. Lord Lamond wants her up there as a guest today. I was just telling her that next thing he'll be asking her to marry him.'

'For goodness sake, Archie,' Isla cried out angrily, 'don't be ridiculous.' She had no wish for her business, or anything private about herself, to be discussed in front of this man.

'You don't belong there,' Hudson said with a sneer. 'You didn't before and you don't now.'

She stamped her foot in fury. 'How dare you say that? What do you know about me? Absolutely nothing! I lived very happily in Kirklee Castle and if the chance arose I would gladly live there again.'

Hudson shook his head. 'Lamond may be a fine fellow, I can't deny that, but you know he's not man enough for you.'

'What? Lord Lamond? Apart from gambling and the business of the canal, you don't know a thing about him. I do. He's a most courageous gentleman.'

Hudson grinned at her. 'Of that I have no doubt. But that's not what I meant.'

Isla felt her cheeks burn. He was an impertinent, arrogant man. At that moment she hated him. She turned away from him and went through to the kitchen, her heart pounding and her legs weak and trembling.

Damn Hudson, she thought. If there was one thing she had learnt since leaving Kirklee it was that determination and confidence made anything possible. Look what she had achieved at The Glasgow Bell, she told herself. Fortune had smiled on her then, so why not this time? She decided there and then that if there was any chance of becoming mistress of Kirklee, she would not let it slip away.

As she waited for the carriage she tried to calm herself. At last it arrived and to her embarrassment, almost everyone in the inn came rushing through to the kitchen to announce the fact in great excitement.

'Come on, hen,' Archie cried out, 'that's it waiting for you. Hurry up.'

Despite the embarrassment of having to pass Hudson in the bar with every one of the staff of The Glasgow Bell crowding after her, she couldn't help sharing their excitement and delight. A liveried footman assisted her into the carriage, then he climbed up the outside of the coach and perched stiff-backed on his high seat. The coachman flicked at the horses and the coach moved off.

Isla spread out the shiny green satin of her skirts. Then, relaxing back, she opened her fan and leisurely wafted it to and fro in front of her flushed cheeks. She must remember, she kept telling herself in an effort to keep calm, that there was nothing daunting about

Kirklee Castle. She had lived there before. She knew practically every corner of the place. She had no need to feel nervous.

If Isla felt anxious, it was certainly not visible when she reached Kirklee. Alighting from the carriage, she graciously accepted the assistance of the footman, before sweeping towards the familiar iron-studded door and waiting with some impatience as the bell jangled inside. They knew that she was due to arrive. The door should have been open and one of the maids ready to receive her, or one of the footmen, or even Mrs McGregor, the housekeeper.

It was the cheeky Effie who opened the door. With the help of the housekeeper, she had been reinstated at Kirklee since Lady Lamond's death.

'Hello,' she said.

Isla gave her a haughty look.

'Where is his Lordship?'

'In the lower drawing room,' Effie said, still quite perky.

'Well,' Isla said, 'don't just stand there. Take me to him.'

Effie hesitated, surprise registering on her face. Then she turned and made her way along the corridor towards the drawing room. There she opened the door and Isla swept past her. Lord Lamond rose from his seat and came towards her, hands out-stretched in welcome.

'My dear Isla, it is so good to see you back where you belong. I had always regretted the circumstances under which you departed.'

Isla felt a rush of warmth towards him for saying that, especially in front of Effie. He turned to the maid then. 'That will be all, Effie.' Effie had been standing inside the doorway, agape with interest. Suddenly coming to herself, she hastily retreated, shutting the door behind her. Lord Lamond bent over Isla's hand and kissed it.

'You always look beautiful, Isla, but never more so than you do today. It seems to me that you have a flush of happiness on your face. Am I right in thinking it is because you are happy to return here to Kirklee Castle?'

'Oh, indeed, my Lord, that is so. I once regarded this as my home and I was very happy here. The old Earl was like a father to me.'

Lord Lamond smiled. 'Do sit down, my dear. What you say is indeed true, but I thank God that you are not in fact any blood relation of mine.'

Isla raised a brow. Her expression took on a part-defensive, part-defiant look.

'Oh, why's that?' she asked. 'Is it that I'm not good enough to be one of your family?'

He laughed then. 'Still as touchy as ever. You misread my meaning. You surely have realised by now that my feelings towards you are not those that would be suitable for a brother.'

'Oh.' She relaxed then, flushing a little and lowering her eyes. 'I see.'

'I hope you do, my dear. I think we've known each other for long enough now to enable us to be frank and not to waste any more time. I must speak openly – I have always admired you Isla, for your boldness as well as your beauty. Even when my wife was still alive, although of course I could not speak of it then. That is why I wanted you to come here today, to talk to you in the kind of privacy that we could never have in The Glasgow Bell.'

'I see,' she repeated, at a loss for what else to say. She felt taken aback by what now seemed a sudden turn of events.

'What I am going to say may seem a little presumptuous, some would say hasty and ill-considered. There will be those who will think me mad to even consider such a thing. But, as you well know Isla, I am a man who knows his own mind. I don't give a damn for the opinion of those who mean nothing to me.'

Isla listened attentively, hardly daring to believe all this was really happening.

'I want you to think seriously about this, Isla. I don't want an answer now. We shall drink a dish of tea and talk about other things, and then after you return to The Glasgow Bell, I want you to think about the question I'm going to ask you. Will you, my dear Isla, do me the honour of becoming my wife? I have thought long and hard about this. My late wife Dorothy, God rest her soul, was a fine woman, but I married her because it was expected. There was no passion in it. With you, Isla, it would be so very different.'

Despite the fact that Isla had dreamed of this, despite the fact that Archie had so confidently prophesied this question being asked, she felt as if it was still a dream. She couldn't believe her ears and she was so happy, so overcome with joy, she thought that she would faint with it.

'Now,' Lord Lamond said, 'I shall ring for Mrs McGregor to bring our tea.'

CHAPTER TWENTY-NINE

With a supreme effort, Isla maintained a calm and dignified demeanour all through that first visit to Kirklee. Even in the carriage on her return to The Glasgow Bell, she kept her poise. She allowed the footman to assist her from the carriage and walked into the hostelry, head held high, passing through the bar which was by now busy with customers. She arrived in the kitchen and as soon as she did so, she gave a loud whoop of joy, lifted her skirts and leapt wildly around, with a great show of white stockings and green satin shoes. All the serving wenches laughed until the tears were streaming down their cheeks. Molly tutted and shook her head, but was hard put to conceal her smiles.

Hearing the commotion, Archie came running through from the bar. 'You've done it, hen, you've done it,' he cried out. 'I knew it! I knew you would get him to ask you. When's the big wedding to be then?'

'I haven't given my answer yet,' Isla said. 'He told me to go home and think about it.'

'Think about it?' Archie said incredulously. 'What's there to think about?'

'I'm just telling you what he said. I didn't want to seem unladylike and rush the thing.'

'Oh aye, you're quite right, hen. We'll have to play this careful. You'll have to be ladylike, that's true. So stop that louping about like a mad thing and roaring out like one of the navvies. If you're going to be the new Lady Lamond, you'll have to stop acting like a wild thing. You'll have to learn to change your ways, Isla, or you'll put him off.'

Isla tossed her skirts down. 'Don't worry. You should have seen me up there today. A perfect lady, I was. Nobody could be more dignified, I can tell you.'

'Aye, well,' Archie said, 'just you remember to stay like that.'

'I know a lot more than you how you're

supposed to behave among the so-called quality.' Isla replied haughtily.

Archie looked affronted. 'What do you mean saying things like that? So-called? What do you mean, so-called? They *are* the quality.'

'Listen, Archie. I know them, and it's all just manners and show. Inside, they're no better than me, or even you. Some of the gentlemen and the lords that I've met – well, haven't you seen for yourself in the gambling room – they could drink even you under the table. The only difference is they have servants to carry them home and put them to bed and they're in no danger of waking up penniless because of their drinking, or even their gambling for that matter.'

Archie shook his head.

'You're an awful lassie. I've always said that – you're an awful lassie,' he repeated. 'But never mind all that, when are you going to give him your answer?'

She gave a little twirl of excitement. 'He's taking me to Glasgow next week. He's going to book rooms at the Saracen's Head. We're to attend the dancing assembly.' She gave another whoop of joy. 'That'll be one in the eye for Mr and Mrs Menzies and all the rest of them there. Oh, I can hardly wait.'

'Aye,' Archie chortled, bright-eyed and vigorously rubbing his hands in delight, 'aye, they've always been too big for their boots, that lot. They need taking down a peg or two.'

'I'll have to see about getting a new dress made right away,' Isla said.

'A week's not much time,' Molly remarked worriedly.

'It's all right. I know the mantua maker who used to make all the clothes at Kirklee for the ladies. She'll have been hard pressed to earn anything since they've all gone. She'll be glad of any work I give her and she's two daughters who'll no doubt be glad to help as well.

'Money's no object, remember,' Archie said. 'You'll need to look the part. I can hardly wait to spread the news. Near enough father-in-law of a lord! Will that make me a lord as well?'

'Don't be daft,' Isla said. 'You have to be born a lord to be a lord. And don't you dare go spreading any news until I tell you. Lord Lamond has to know my answer first, not a whole crowd of navvies.'

'Aye, aye, right enough, hen. But can we no' just give a wee hint to that Mr Hudson. Say what you like about him, but he's always been keen on you. He would have you in a minute, if you would let him.'

'Well, I'm not going to let him.' Her happiness and excitement suddenly and unaccountably deflated at the mention of Hudson's name. What was it about him that always seemed to throw her thoughts into turmoil?

'Aye, well, he'll stop pestering you when he knows you're promised to Lord Lamond. By God, he'll have to.'

'Well,' Isla hesitated, 'maybe if you get the chance to mention it to him discreetly, it might help right enough.'

'Aye, all right, hen. Trust me, I'll be very discreet and casual like.'

She couldn't work that night. She couldn't sleep for hours either. Next morning she awoke early and as soon as memories of the day before crowded in on her consciousness, she leapt from the bed, unable to contain her joy. She whirled around the room like a dervish. She wanted to fly up into the air and out of the window and over the countryside, so intoxicating was her sense of triumph. Then in the midst of her happiness a thought occurred to her. She would have to be a mother to little Theresa. How would she cope with taking on the child of Dorothy Lamond, a woman she had thoroughly detested?

Casting this problem aside for the time being, she flung on some clothes and ran downstairs, and out of the back door. She raced across the yard, then away over the fields, through the woods until, exhausted, she crumpled down in a clearing beside a pool. The golden rays of the sun caught her uncombed auburn hair and seemed to set it on fire.

She tugged her fingers through its thick mass, then impulsively she decided to wash it in the cool sparkling water of the pond. She pulled her blouse down and over her shoulders to her waist. She bent forward and, kneeling on a smooth stone, dipped her head to the water. Her hair swirled in the pool like spilled wine, flowing in sensuous curves as the water lapped at the edges of the stone. Eventually, her hair thoroughly washed, she swung herself upright. Her hair arched upwards as she threw her head back, spraying droplets of water skywards, the individual drops sparkling in the sun like diamonds thrown away with careless abandon.

Then after squeezing as much water as she could from her long tresses, she scrambled up and danced around shaking her head and making her hair fly about and her breasts bounce.

Suddenly there was a clapping sound. She stopped in her tracks. There, a few yards away from her, was the tall figure of David Hudson grinning at her and clapping as if she had been performing some entertainment for his pleasure. Shock was quickly chased by rage and indignation.

'You bastard,' she shouted at him. 'You've been doing it again.'

He laughed. 'Doing what?'

'You know perfectly well! You've been watching me.'

'Perhaps I should to do more than just watch you,' he said moving towards her.

'Don't you dare touch me,' she screamed at him. 'I hate you, I told you that before. I hate you.' Then, because her words had no effect on him whatsoever and he continued to advance towards her, she turned and ran away with the speed of a gazelle.

CHAPTER THIRTY

Isla was no match for Hudson's powerful physique. Effortlessly, it seemed, he caught up with her, grabbed her waist, swung her round to face him and brought his mouth down hard over hers.

She punched at him with both fists with every ounce of her strength. She kicked him too but only succeeded in hurting her bare feet against his high leather boots. She struggled to twist her face away from his, angry at herself to the point of tears for the strange pleasurable sensations that his mouth was awakening in her.

In desperation, she brought her knee up into his groin. With a curse, he bent forward clutching at himself, making her stumble back, lose her balance and fall down onto the grassy bank. He dropped down beside her and grabbed her by the shoulders, his face white with anger. Then, as he looked at her, the anger in his face faded, and his eyes darkened with passion. His mouth covered hers again but softly. His lips moved over hers caressingly, then gradually he opened her mouth and his tongue explored inside it. Her struggles changed from trying to push him away to clutching him to her.

She moaned with the pleasure of him and instinctively arched her body against his. Suddenly, she heard him whisper close to her ear,

'I always knew you wanted me.'

Her anger immediately returned. This time, however, she didn't need to fight to push him away from her. He rolled onto his back, laughing.

'Admit it, my dear. You were never meant to be mistress of Kirklee.'

She scrambled to her feet, pulling her blouse up over her naked breasts. He watched her, his arms folded behind his head.

'I'm not going to allow you to spoil things for me,' she said, anger blazing in her eyes.

'God forbid,' he said. 'I'm trying to improve things for you.'

'And how may I ask,' she sneered, 'could you possibly do that.'

He grinned up at her. 'By marrying you, of course.'

'What conceit!' she gasped. 'Well, I can tell you right now, if that's supposed to be a proposal of marriage, my answer to you is no! Do you hear me? No, I said. Now just leave me alone from now on.'

With that, she turned and ran back towards The Bell. She had been so happy, so full of joy before. Now she was upset and worse, much worse, confused. She longed for the calming influence of Lord Lamond – his unshakeable, total self-assurance. Where she had always had to prove herself and make her own way, he was so secure in the knowledge that he was one of the landed aristocracy. She knew that not every noble lord deserved the respect and admiration that their position accorded them. But Lord Lamond – like his father, the old Earl, before him – deserved every ounce of respect, and not only admiration but love. She would never forget what a gentleman the old Earl had been to her. As well as being her protector and so kind and generous towards her, he had treated her like a lady. Now she was to be a lady to Lord Lamond. A lady fit to receive the honour of being his wife. She could have wept with gratitude and pride. Nothing, she tried to convince herself, nothing or no-one was going to prevent her from fulfilling her destiny.

Not only that, she resolved to fill this position of honour with such perfection that it would be as if she had been born into the aristocracy instead of a hovel in one of the stinking wynds of Glasgow.

Lord Lamond had gone to Edinburgh for a few days to attend to matters of business and so he did not attend the gambling session that evening. Isla looked in to see that the other gentlemen were enjoying their game and after chatting to them for a few minutes, she returned to the corridor. She was just about to mount the stairs to her room when David Hudson entered through the back door.

'Isla,' he called to her. 'Just a moment.'

She took a deep breath. 'Did I not make myself perfectly clear this morning?'

'Yes, but I didn't,' he said. 'I must talk to you in private. Let's go in here.'

He took her arm and forced her across and into the breakfast room. She violently tugged her arm free of him.

'I don't want to talk to you. I've nothing to say to you.'

'Just listen to me for a few minutes. I know how difficult your situation must be. On the surface, it looks a wonderful opportunity to become Lady Lamond and live in Kirklee Castle.'

'On the surface?' she said. 'What do you mean, on the surface? It *is* a wonderful opportunity, and on any and every level.'

'But what do you feel about him?'

'That is none of your business.'

'I'm making it my business. I love you and I want to marry you.'

'Love! Love!' Isla gave a dismissive flick of her hand. 'My mother loved Archie Anderson and look where it got her. Into an early grave.'

'Did she? I wonder about that. My guess is she decided to marry Archie Anderson for much the same reason as you've decided to marry Lord Lamond.'

Isla laughed contemptuously. 'That's absolutely ridiculous! What nonsense is this.'

'She was a poor widow woman, I've heard.'

Isla shrugged. 'Well, there's no shame in that.'

'I'm not talking about shame,' Hudson said impatiently. 'And don't try to pretend to me that you don't know what I'm talking about. This place must have seemed every bit as good as a castle to your mother.'

Isla felt a secret stab of fear. She couldn't bear to listen to him any more. Thoughts of her mother were too painful. She made to turn away but one of Hudson's big hands stopped her.

'Don't go,' he said. 'There's more to be said yet.'

'There's no comparison,' Isla cried out desperately. 'No comparison at all between my mother's situation and mine. I'm not in poor circumstances. I have a good home here and this is now a very profitable business.'

'Isla, listen to me. I will provide you with a good home. I will build you a mansion house. I know the very spot, not many miles from here.'

'No, no, no,' she cried out in desperation. 'Do not do this to me, please. I could be so happy with Lord Lamond.'

Hudson shook his head. 'You are happy with the idea of being Lady Lamond but how long will that kind of happiness last? The days of the aristocracy are numbered. The charmed life they lead now will disappear – and their noble lordships along with it. Have you not heard what is happening in France? The future belongs to industry and commerce, to those with ability and ambition. To people like you and me, Isla. You are in love with what Lamond stands for, not the man himself.'

Isla hardly knew what to say. She had not realised he was a man of such dangerous passion. Could she have been wrong about him?

'You don't know how I feel. How can you?' She whispered.

He looked at her in silence for a moment, then he said quietly, 'When I look at you, when I touch you, when I kiss you, when I hold you, that's how I know.'

With an effort, Isla gathered all her earnestly practised dignity around her. 'You are mistaken, Mr Hudson,' she said coldly. Then she turned and walked from the room.

CHAPTER THIRTY-ONE

The mantua maker and her two daughters came to The Glasgow Bell and stayed in one of the spare bedrooms so that they could work continuously on Isla's dress. It was to be an open robe in white muslin embroidered in silver, with silver buttons to hold the gathered sleeves. Isla went to Glasgow to buy a pair of silver satin shoes to complement the dress.

It was while she was in the town, and just coming down from the High Street, that she saw a crowd of excited people streaming along the Trongate. Before she knew what was happening, she found herself caught up with them and swept along. It was when the crowd reached the Tolbooth jail that Isla began to realise what was happening. She could hardly believe her eyes. It seemed so incredible.

At the head of the crowd, being dragged along by the guard and now hustled into the Tolbooth, was the barely recognisable figure of Miss Esther Nichol. At first Isla thought she must be mistaken. After all, Miss Nichol had always been very genteel and fashionably turned out. Even her hair had always been carefully coiffured. The sight that met Isla's eyes now was of a poor scrap of a woman, her hair dishevelled, her clothes filthy and torn. Isla pushed forward to get a closer look and just before the woman disappeared inside, their eyes met and Isla saw the tragic look of recognition.

She felt shocked. She was speechless for a minute or two, then she turned to the woman nearest to her and said, 'What has happened? What's that poor woman supposed to have done?'

'Haven't you heard?' the woman said. 'It's all over the town.'

Isla shook her head.

'Well,' the woman went on, obviously eager for a gossip, 'there's this gentleman, Mr Raeburn, and they say he used to be a neighbour of that woman. Nichol is her name. Esther Nichol. And do you know what that terrible woman suggested to him?'

Isla shook her head again.

'That she would give him poison to kill his wife! She's a right witch, that woman. They say she makes up poisons. Of course, Mr Raeburn was horrified and refused. But worse than that, do you know what came out?'

'No,' Isla managed, unable though to think of anything that could be worse.

'She had already poisoned somebody else. Lady Lamond, no less. Fancy, such wickedness! And you'd never have thought it to look at her, the timid wee thing.'

Isla felt quite faint with astonishment as well as horror.

'What do you think's going to happen to her?'

'She deserves to be burned at the stake,' the woman said. 'The chances are they'll just hang her.'

Isla couldn't help feeling sorry for the woman. She had often felt like murdering Lady Lamond herself, and she remembered how Esther had been the only one who had been kind to her when she was forced to leave Kirklee. After the crowd had dispersed and gone their separate ways, she waited outside the Tolbooth.

Eventually, she managed to speak to one of the guards and persuade him, with much fluttering of eyelashes and coquettish glances, to allow her to have a few words with the prisoner.

She found Miss Nichol crouched on the stone floor in the corner of a gloomy cell. The woman was trembling violently and her eyes were huge in a sickly grey face.

'Oh, Isla,' she quavered. 'They say that they're going to whip me through the streets tomorrow and then hang me for all to see. But worst of all, was his betrayal, Isla. Mr Raeburn betrayed me. That is what I cannot bear.'

'Why did you tell him about Lady Lamond?' Isla asked. 'Surely that was very foolish of you.'

'He was afraid to take the potion I was offering him. He was making the excuse that it wouldn't work. It was only as a last resort I told him that indeed it would work because I'd used it before. He had told me so much about his unhappiness with Alice Raeburn and what an awful woman she was and how he would so gladly be rid of her, I thought–' she shook her head –'I thought...' Her voice trailed away.

'I'm sorry,' Isla said. 'I really am, Miss Nichol. If I could do something to help you, I would, but there isn't anything. It's too late now.'

Miss Nichol looked up quickly, eagerly. 'No, no, it isn't too late, Isla. Oh, please, help me. I'm so afraid. I'm terrified of tomorrow. You are the only one who can help me now. I beg you, do me this one last service.'

'But what can I do?' Isla asked.

Miss Nichol struggled to her feet and ran across to clutch at Isla's hands. 'Isla, you know I was living with the ladies? Well, I had a few phials of herbal mixtures. I always carry them with me in case of any maladies that anyone might have. Bring them to me, Isla, please. And my Bible. Tell the ladies that I want my Bible. And when you come back, if you tell them that it's the Bible you're bringing me, the guards will allow that. They cannot refuse the Bible to one who stands condemned as I do.'

Isla hesitated. 'The herbal potions, will they calm you? Will they be of some comfort?'

'Oh yes, Isla. Remember when I gave one to you, how it soothed you? I'm so terrified of tomorrow, Isla. I desperately need your help.'

'All right, then,' Isla said. 'I'll go right away and come straight back.'

'Oh thank you, Isla, thank you.'

Isla left the cell and returned outside. She felt upset and not just because of Miss Nichol. She was thinking of Lord Lamond as well. How would he be feeling? What sort of emotions had all this stirred up in him? What angers, what griefs, what regrets? He would be home from Edinburgh now and would no doubt appear in the gambling room this evening. She had been looking forward to his return. Now she thought of it with dread.

Thankfully, the ladies were not at home when she arrived at their tenement flat, but Teenie the maid asked her in after she said who she was and the purpose of her visit.

'Och, it's a terrible business,' Teenie said,

'but we canna deny her God's word.'

And so Isla collected the Bible and the phials without any trouble and returned as quickly as she could to the Tolbooth jail. She was allowed to enter with the Bible and handed it over with the phials to an eager and pathetically grateful Miss Nichol.

As they said their goodbyes, Isla impulsively gave the older woman a kiss and an affectionate hug.

'May God help you to have courage, Miss Nichol.'

Out in the street once again, Isla made her way towards the road leading to The Glasgow Bell. She had got the stage from the hostelry into the town, but had no option but to walk back. She was glad in a way. She needed time to think and the exercise as she strode along helped release some of the distress she had been feeling.

Once back in The Glasgow Bell, she washed her face in cold water, combed her hair and changed her dress. She was just about to go downstairs when there was a tap at her door. She called 'Enter' and the door opened to reveal Lord Lamond. She was glad that her practice in ladylike behaviour had not deserted her. A few months ago, she would have been more likely to have bawled something impertinent rather than the polite 'Enter' that she had just given.

'My Lord,' she said in some surprise. He

had never come upstairs before.

'Have you heard?' Lord Lamond asked.

She nodded. 'It must have been a terrible shock to you, my Lord.'

He sauntered past her into the room. 'Yes, indeed, Isla. A shocking business altogether. To think that someone who shared my own home as a member of my own family could do such a thing. It is almost beyond belief. I trust you'll accompany me to Glasgow tomorrow?' Then, seeing her slightly puzzled look, he added, 'To witness the hanging. I am mightily looking forward to it.'

She hesitated, but only for a second. 'Of course. When do you propose to leave?'

'I will call for you with the carriage at nine o'clock. They are going to whip her through the streets first and although I would dearly like to witness that, there will be such crowds, it will be difficult for us. Better that we should wait in the coach at the Tolbooth.'

'I'll be ready at nine o'clock,' Isla told him.

He gave a small bow and left, spending the rest of the evening with his gentlemen friends in the gambling room. They stayed very late and she didn't wait up to see them off. She was tired after the walk from Glasgow.

Nevertheless, she found she couldn't sleep. She lay wide-eyed and very much awake. Every now and again, she would hear the mournful sound of a horn which gave warning that a flat-bottomed scow or some other vessel was navigating the canal. The small light that they carried at the bow, which by law had to be kept burning from sunset to sunrise, cast eerie shadows across Isla's bedroom wall. If she listened intently, she could hear the gentle lapping of the water. She lay like that for many hours, trying not to think of Miss Nichol.

CHAPTER THIRTY-TWO

The Lamond equipage was not the only one heading for the town of Glasgow that morning. Isla spotted the Raeburn carriage and quite a few others belonging to the local gentry. Horses were prancing along, ladies were waving lace handkerchiefs from carriage windows in cheerful greeting to one another. There was a carnival air reminiscent of the yearly Glasgow Fair and all its rude hilarity and merry-making.

Ploughmen and dairy maids and other country workers were also crowding along the roads on foot, on horseback and in lumbering horse-drawn carts. The air was alive with talk and laughter.

Isla sat stiff-backed in her seat, pale and silent. Lord Lamond did not seem to notice, or probably took for granted now her more subdued and ladylike demeanour. He kept returning greetings from other travellers with a raise of his hand or a tilt of his head, and a pleasant smile. At one point, the Raeburn coach drew near and Alice Raeburn stuck her head out of the window, knocking her huge-brimmed straw hat, much decorated with bunched and trailing ribbon, slightly askew.

'A happy day, Lord Lamond,' she called out. 'Justice is being done at last.'

'Indeed, madam, indeed,' Lord Lamond called back to her.

Isla had heard in fact that there was to be more than one hanging that day. Charlie Mitchell was to be hanged for street robbery and Neil Stephens for forgery. There was another woman too, Aggie McAulay, for theft and the notorious Malcolm Crosbie was to be hanged and beheaded for high treason. No wonder, Archie had said, that the Tolbooth steeple was attracting so many folk that day, all intent on enjoying the spectacle.

The weather also played its part. Already the sun was shining on the revellers, and in the midst of one group a man was scraping vigorously at a fiddle. Several people around him, delighted to be freed from their day's labour, were louping about in a happy dance. The streets of Glasgow were already crowded and noisy. Some men and women, children too, had already taken up vantage points at open tenement windows.

When Lord Lamond's carriage reached the Tolbooth, he leaned from the window and called out to one of the guards, 'Has the Nichol woman had her whipping yet? Is she ready for the hanging?'

The guard looked embarrassed. 'I'm sorry, my Lord, the truth is when we went to fetch her earlier this morning, we found the woman already dead.'

Lord Lamond's face darkened.

'How can that be? How did she die?'

'We do not know for sure, my Lord. We thought she was sleeping at first and gave her a good shaking. As we did so, some empty phials fell from her clothing and they're saying that she poisoned herself. Perhaps this is the best justice, my Lord, dying by the same means as she caused the death of your wife.'

'I am sorry to say I do not agree,' Lord Lamond said coldly. 'I came to see the Nichol woman hanged, and see her hanged I will.'

'Now, my Lord?'

'Now!'

The guard bowed. 'I will fetch the body, my Lord.'

Lord Lamond leaned back on his seat. 'They shall hear more of this. She ought to have been searched. She ought to have been watched.'

As a dreadful realisation dawned on her, Isla spoke up.

'Do not be too hard on the guards, my Lord. They have much to do and many prisoners.' From the corner of her eye, Isla saw the guard dragging out the inert body of Miss Nichol. It was shocking to see the sorry state that such a woman had been reduced to. She was glad that Miss Nichol knew nothing of her present terrible humiliation. Isla even forgave her for tricking her into bringing what she now knew had been poison.

The body was unceremoniously strung up and hung from the gibbet like a broken doll, spinning gently in the breeze. Few in the assembled crowd could see the point of this gesture, but many simply felt cheated of their rightful entertainment. For Isla it was a sickening sight from which she quickly averted her eyes. After a few minutes, the guard went to cut the body down but Lord Lamond called out to him, 'Leave her there a while longer, so that everyone can witness her shame.'

'But my Lord,' the guard faltered, 'there are other prisoners...'

'Let them wait, I am quite certain they will not complain.' Lord Lamond said. Then he tapped the roof of the coach with his gold-topped cane, signalling the coachman to move off. The horses pranced forward, scattering the crowd in all directions, as people tried to avoid the animals' hooves.

'I am most annoyed,' Lord Lamond said eventually, 'that the creature escaped the whipping.'

After a moment, Isla said, 'You are very bitter, my Lord.'

Lord Lamond looked round at her. 'Do you forget, my dear Isla, that my wife died in agony because of that woman?'

'No, of course I do not forget, my Lord. I am only thinking of your peace of mind, as I'm sure Lady Lamond would if she were here. All she ever wanted was for you to be happy.'

He sighed, then nodded. 'You are right, of course. I must look to the future now, not the past.' Turning, he lifted Isla's hand and touched it to his lips. 'And the future is ours, my dear lady.'

Isla's spirits lifted slightly, partly because he had called her 'lady' and partly because she was pleasantly reminded of her future life at Kirklee Castle.

'How is your little daughter, my Lord?'

Lord Lamond shrugged. 'She appears well enough. But I am sure she will fare much better with you to care for her.' Then, after a minute or two of silence, he said, 'I cannot bear to be parted from you today, Isla. Come home with me to Kirklee.'

She glanced round at him. 'I would be happy to do so, my Lord, as long as I am assured that I spend the night in my old room.'

He smiled. 'Ah, I cannot tempt you to share my bed this evening then?'

'Time enough,' Isla said, 'when we are married.'

'So! I have your answer at last! Well, let it be soon then. Let us set the date for this summer.'

She returned his smile. 'That will suit me very well.' And so it was settled. She relaxed back against the cushions, still surprisingly low in spirits. It had been a difficult day and, as if fate was determined to make it even more difficult, just then the Raeburn coach came alongside and Alice Raeburn stuck her head out and called over to them,

'You will come to dinner with us. Do!'

As Lord Lamond hesitated, she called out, 'I refuse to take no for an answer, Lord Lamond. We will race on ahead and be waiting at our door to welcome you.' Then she shouted up at her coachman, 'Faster, can't you.' With a jerk the coach accelerated and she was suddenly jolted back onto her seat and her hat knocked forward over her face. Isla couldn't help giggling. Lord Lamond laughed too.

'A dreadful woman, isn't she? I don't think much of Hamish Raeburn either, but...' he shrugged, 'they are neighbours. It is as well not to offend them. Anyway, I believe they have a prodigiously good cook.'

The mention of Hamish Raeburn caused Isla's smile to vanish. Despicable, weak traitor of a man, she thought. He had obviously been playing with Miss Nichol's affections and then – coward that he was – he had betrayed her. He could just have refused the poison and left it at that. But no, he had panicked. She could just imagine it. Fearful for his own safety and reputation, he had run to his wife in mock indignation and righteousness and he had betrayed Miss Nichol. Once she was mistress of Kirklee Castle, she would give the Raeburns short shrift.

Meantime she had to tread carefully. She had to accompany Lord Lamond to the Raeburns' mansion house with as much good grace as she could muster.

She had to sit with the Raeburns at their long dinner table. It was loaded with a large dish of soup, composed of mutton mixed with oatmeal flour, onions, parsley and peas. There was a dish of black pudding too, made with bullock's blood and barley flour seasoned with pepper and ginger. Another dish was piled with slices of beef and yet another with roasted mutton and potatoes done in the juice. There were cucumbers and ginger, pickled with vinegar, and a pudding made of barley meal, cream and currants cooked in dripping.

Mrs Raeburn's high, aggressive, affected

voice barely ceased during the whole of the meal. Hamish Raeburn was even quieter than usual in his wife's company. He fidgeted constantly, eyes furtively averted from everyone, a vague apologetic smile flitting every now and again over his face.

Isla longed to throw her plate of soup over him. She longed to knock him off his chair with a few well-aimed punches. She wanted to shout at him, 'You shifty, weak, little, pathetic excuse for a man!' However, she managed to control herself and just fix Mr Raeburn with an icy and unwavering stare.

Afterwards, she even managed to say a polite and dignified goodbye to both the Raeburns before leaving in Lord Lamond's coach. Later still, after a pleasant evening with Lamond at Kirklee chatting and playing cards, she lay in bed in her old room and tried to feel proud of herself for her ladylike behaviour.

It was now obvious that Lord Lamond held her in very high regard indeed. Her life was working out splendidly. She had come a long way and she was going to go even further.

But strangely, all the other feelings she'd recently enjoyed had also become subdued, indeed had disappeared altogether. The impulse to dance around the room with happiness, the longing to fly high in the air and out over the countryside in an ecstasy of triumph and joy. She felt none of these things. Closing her eyes, she lay very still in the silence of the castle. She missed the lapping and the splashing of the canal water, the big plodding feet of the Clydesdale horses, the gabbarts and scows and other vessels that they pulled along. She missed the sounds of horns and trumpets, all the vibrant life of the canal and the rousing good-humour of the navvies. God knows, she even missed that old fool Archie Anderson! But more than anything, she missed The Glasgow Bell.

CHAPTER THIRTY-THREE

Lamond was going hunting the next day. Many guests were expected and he wanted Isla to stay, but she made her excuses and persuaded him to have the coach take her back to The Glasgow Bell first thing in the morning.

When she arrived back at the hostelry, David Hudson was having breakfast. She looked in at the breakfast room. Another couple, who had stayed overnight, were also enjoying the meal. Isla wished everyone good morning and the couple returned her greeting, but Hudson gave her a dark scowl. She retreated from the room in annoyance.

As usual, he could immediately change her mood from the heights to the depths. She felt on edge now, unable to concentrate properly on what she had intended to do for the rest of the day.

She had been looking forward to having a talk with Molly and answering the string of questions that she knew would be forth-coming about what had happened in Glasgow, and also how she had got on at Kirklee. Now, instead, when Molly greeted her with an eager 'How did you get on? What happened?', she just shrugged and said, 'I got on perfectly well. I'm going out for a breath of fresh air before I do anything.'

With that, she left the surprised Molly and went out through the front door and down onto the tow path. She stood for a few minutes watching one of the thirty nine locks of the canal rush into life, a sparkling waterfall in the morning sun. In the other direction, in the distance, she could see a crowd of navvies puddling. This, she had learned, was the roughest, toughest and most arduous work executed by the navvies, entailing much heavy and hazardous digging.

Isla had always admired the navvies' skill and capacity for hard work. Although Hudson was a contractor and a shareholder in the canal company, she had often heard his men say that there wasn't one job they did that he could not tackle himself. Indeed, she'd sometimes seen him, bare-chested and wearing the high-laced boots of the navvies, digging alongside the men as they attempted a particularly difficult job – where there was a bend or a deviation from the straight.

Afterwards he'd come into the bar room and order a tankard of ale. She always tried to avoid looking at his tanned skin and muscular chest. The weathered skin of his face was equally disturbing because it somehow made his dark eyes darker and his black hair blacker. Sometimes she thought that there was something satanic about him. His stare could be so knowledgeable, so powerfully intense, that it seemed as if he was penetrating her clothing and savouring her nakedness.

She closed her eyes to try to blot out thoughts of him. She struggled instead to think about Lord Lamond – cool, elegant, sophisticated and with a charm that every lady found delightful. Men admired him too. He was an entertaining companion, excellent at both the hunt and the shoot. His skill at the card table was also admired, as well as his calm nonchalance in the face of heavy losses.

She opened her eyes to see a tall-masted vessel floating gracefully along. Two giant horses were slowly towing it. The animals passed so close to her that she smelled the sweat of them. She thought of Kirklee and how she would soon be mistress of the castle, yet no matter how hard she tried, she could not think of it as her home. With a sigh, she turned and went back indoors.

CHAPTER THIRTY-FOUR

David Hudson strolled in to join the gentlemen in the gambling room, dressed like a gentleman himself in his white breeches, cut-away black coat, high turned over collar, ruffled shirt front and short waistcoat.

Isla recognised his deep-throated laughter among the laughter of the others and felt uneasy. The next day, when he was alone in the breakfast room, she went in and stood in front of him.

'Why do you keep coming to the gambling room? I thought I made my feelings plain, sir. You are no longer welcome here.'

He gave her an amused look. 'Why not?'

'You know perfectly well why not,' Isla cried out in exasperation.

He shrugged. 'Your gambling room has acquired the reputation of being the best place to enjoy a wager for miles around, and I for one have reason to celebrate. We're starting on the last section of the Glasgow branch and there's a plan afoot to extend it to the new village of Port Dundas. Port Dundas,' he repeated in some satisfaction, 'named in honour of Lord Dundas, governor of the canal company.' He paused for a moment, then, with a wicked glint in his eye, continued,

'You thought, of course, that my coming here had only to do with you.'

She whirled round on him again. 'I can assure you, sir, I thought nothing of the kind!'

He helped himself to a mouthful of food and chewed at it for a while before saying,

'In truth the reason for my spending so much time here was to allow me to observe our noble friend Lord Lamond, to see if I could find any other attraction for you apart from his wealth and position.'

'What impertinence!' Isla gasped. 'It has nothing to do with you.'

'Oh yes it has,' Hudson said. 'The time for pretence is over! You should be marrying me. You know that as well as I do. It is only a matter of time before you admit it. And I can wait. Indeed, I will wait as long as it takes for you to come to your senses!'

'I have never in my life,' Isla said, 'come across such an incredible conceit. I have never once given you a single word of encouragement. Quite the reverse, sir!'

She waited for a reply but none was forthcoming. Hudson was enjoying the rest of his breakfast. She made to move away again but found herself unable to leave the room without asking him,

'And what is your considered opinion of Lord Lamond then?'

'I confess I have a great liking for the man. He has much nerve at the tables. I admire a good loser. He is in fact an excellent all-round sportsman, but, typical of his class, he's never done an honest day's work in his life.'

'He doesn't need to work,' Isla said. 'He's a wealthy man.'

'True enough,' Hudson agreed, before returning once more to his breakfast.

In exasperation, Isla left the room, banging the door behind her. She was about to lift her skirts and race up the stairs taking them two at a time, then she remembered that she was supposed to behave like a lady. Controlling the urge she gracefully swanned up the stairs, taking her time. Once in the privacy of her bedroom, however, she flung herself on her bed and freely indulged her emotions. She punched at the pillow, kicked her heels and wished with desperate intensity that it was Hudson she was punching and kicking.

Eventually she exhausted herself. She lay still for a time, feeling reluctant to go back downstairs. Probably Hudson would have gone by now but still her reluctance remained.

Perhaps what she needed was a complete change, to get away from The Bell. For too long now, it had been her whole life. The very next time she saw Lamond she would tell him that she had a fancy to stay at Kirklee for a few days. Later, she spoke to him to announce her intention.

'Of course you must. We have a great deal to talk about and plan for. It is time, for instance, that we were planning the details of our wedding.'

'Yes indeed, my Lord,' Isla agreed, and so it was arranged the carriage would call for her the next day.

To celebrate her visit, Lord Lamond invited several of the local gentry to dinner. A hunt was also arranged. The first evening she was at Kirklee, however, she and Lord Lamond were alone together and they spent the time planning their nuptials. The wedding service was to take place in the church at Kirkintilloch, then the rest of the celebrations would be held at Kirklee.

'Nearer the time,' Lord Lamond said, 'you can speak with Mrs McGregor and the cook and tell them what you would like to be served at the wedding feast.' Of all the plans that they discussed, this was the one that took her fancy most. She looked forward to giving Mrs McGregor and the cook their orders. Again that evening, she was back in her old room, but this time her mind was filled with what she and Lord Lamond had been discussing.

The next morning, the local gentry arrived for the hunt. Most of them, she discovered, had robust limbs, fat faces, red noses, and were dressed for the hunt in thick yellowish ancestral buckskins, with brown tops to their boots. And they were so noisy. Even the normal 'A good-day to you, sir' was bawled at the top of their voices. Such a clatter and chatter, such a blaze of red jackets, such a hallooing and horn-blowing and dogs in full-throated chorus. Isla couldn't help thinking that in their own way these men were even more noisy and unruly than the navvies.

Lord Lamond was calm and smiling as he reined his horse round in the midst of it all. His slim elegance in very white, well-made leathers, his intelligent blue eyes, his dignified carriage, all spelled out his aristocratic superiority. None of his companions were on the same social level as him, and it showed.

Only the gentlemen were taking part in the hunt and as soon as they had gone streaming away across the countryside in the wake of a brown and white sea of dogs, the ladies floated back to the house in ripples of muslin and flowered silk. Once inside the castle, the ladies repaired to the drawing room where they sipped tea and nibbled sugared biscuits. Isla found it difficult to contribute to their rather tiresome talk of embroidery, tatting, the next ball in Glasgow and the price of ribbons. They would have been scandalised had she spoken of her own life at The Glasgow Bell.

Later, after the men returned, everyone did justice to the dinner. Indeed, Isla noticed that the appetites of most of the men were gigantic and she couldn't help feeling some distaste. The servants had obviously been well primed and were on their best and most attentive behaviour. Isla also noticed that they were all wearing new and very splendid livery. Lord Lamond clearly did not share his late wife's caution with money.

Kirklee did not have a ballroom but Lord Lamond had ordered two of the largest rooms on the third floor to be transformed into one large area suitable for dancing. The ceiling was very ancient and made of wood so dark as to be almost black, upon which one could just discern coloured shapes and designs painted on the beams. There were no chandeliers hanging from it, but lamp brackets round the white stone walls gave off just enough light. As a result, there was a somewhat eerie atmosphere with the dancers fading in and out of the shadows, like ghosts.

Isla was dressed in floating layers of honey-coloured silk gauze, fastened up at the back in jaunty triple loops of the polonaise. She had paid particular attention to her hair, arranging it in bunches of curls at the nape of her neck which dangled coyly over one ivory shoulder. She felt her gown matched very well with Lord Lamond's golden-brown velvet suit.

After the ball, Lamond had suggested playing cards. She had not joined in herself, but instead watched the game which was played for terrifyingly high stakes. Lord Lamond lost very heavily without showing a ripple on his perfectly cool and calm exterior. He obviously had nerves of steel but Isla couldn't help thinking that it wasn't very wise or even admirable to have as good as thrown away so much money.

No-one arose early next day because of the gambling that had gone on for most of the night. Isla felt particularly lethargic and stayed in bed almost until mid-day. As it turned out, she was the first one to arrive down in the drawing room but as soon as the others appeared, it was announced that after they had eaten they were all going to pay a visit to Glasgow, where there was going to be some special entertainment.

Soon all the coaches were rumbling off towards the town.

CHAPTER THIRTY-FIVE

Isla sat straight-backed in the coach as it passed along the narrow High Street. Lamond had told her that there were going to be several hangings and after they had enjoyed that spectacle, they were going to the Tontine assembly rooms where there was to be a concert.

There was much talk afoot about the new assembly rooms which were going to be built in the Back Cowloan, or Ingram Street as it was now called, but so far the plan hadn't come to anything. Isla viewed the first part of what Lord Lamond called their entertainment with some dismay. She'd never had much of a stomach for hangings, and since Miss Nichol's grisly demise, the very thought filled her with horror.

The coach bumped over the cobbles, allowing her no relief from the tension she felt. All around them people jostled and pushed each other, dogs barked, shopkeepers and street traders shouted out – 'What do you lack? Fresh oysters – penny a lot.' 'Fine candy – good for the cough, colds and shortness of breath.' 'Toasting jacks and toasting forks.' 'Black and white hearted cherries – tuppence a pound. All round and sound.'

The racket of coaches, carts, wagons and trucks drawn by trotting boys seemed to become louder and louder, making Isla's head throb painfully. Soon the crush of carriages became so dense that their horses could no longer press forward. By this time, however, they had reached a position near enough to see the gallows. At least after Lord Lamond had alighted and helped her out and up to a seat beside him on top of the carriage. Isla was more than a little disconcerted to see how he seemed very cheered by this gruesome diversion. There were other coaches, as well as those of their guests who had come with them from Kirklee. Isla could see gentlemen standing on the roofs beside bevvies of ladies. All were finely dressed – the bucks in fashionable hats and high-collared coats, the ladies all powdered and patched and looking very pretty with their trailing mists of scarves and huge hats and flowered, panniered skirts.

Lamond had ordered enough liquor to be brought to satisfy himself and all of his guests and as a result, everyone was in a festive mood as they waited for the entertainment to begin. Everyone except Isla, who did not share their enthusiasm, either for the hangings or the liquor. She began to wonder what she was doing here with people whose enthusiasms seemed so different from her own. This was not at all what she had envisaged when she dreamed of becoming a lady.

Much to Lord Lamond's annoyance, but Isla's relief, they discovered that they had already missed the hanging of two men. There was still however one woman to be hanged and a boy. The boy had to be half-hanged and whipped through the town as a warning against begging.

Eventually a cart appeared on which a woman was tied to a board so that she could not leap over the side. 'She has stolen three loaves of bread,' one of the gentlemen said. The woman looked simple, grinning in return to the laughing crush of spectators, and when the hangman greeted her cheerily, she replied in kind. The crowd and the gentry were highly diverted by this. One half-drunken buck on the next coach nearly swooned with mirth, making his hat fall off and his lady nearly choke with giggles behind her fan.

The boy who waited near the gallows had begun to wail and weep and struggle, and the crowd booed and shouted at him, 'Shame, shame! Coward, coward!'

Lord Lamond said, 'They say he was brought early to see his mother's execution so that it might prove of instruction to him.'

Eyes strained in distress, Isla saw the woman stand on a bucket. Without warning, the hangman's assistant suddenly pulled the bucket away and the woman's body jerked as though the rope would break. The boy, frantic now, was dragged forward, his hysterical sobbing being met by further chants from the gentry of 'Shame, shame! Coward, coward!' The hangman did not trouble to tie the boy, but simply threw him to the ground and, encouraged by the shouts and applause of the crowd, knelt upon the chest of his frantic victim and strangled him with a cord. The cord was removed before the boy was dead, and a bucket of water splashed over him. Then he was tied to the tail of the cart, and while the gentlemen on the surrounding coaches became well-nigh hoarse with admiration, the hangman's assistant began whipping the boy through the streets.

The woman was cut down, then given to her waiting father, who put her in his barrow. Well satisfied, the crowd began to disperse and Lamond helped Isla back inside the coach again, while the old man with the barrow, finding himself in the way of a lady's chariot, was punished by the lady laying her whip to his ears for inconveniencing her so.

At that moment Isla decided one thing for certain. Whether as mistress of Kirklee or landlady of The Glasgow Bell, she would never again willingly witness such scenes of needless, barbaric cruelty. And she could not help but wonder at those around her who seemed to take such pleasure in the misfortune of others.

Meanwhile, beside her, Lamond relaxed back in the coach with a sigh of satisfaction. 'Now my dear, to the Tontine assembly rooms to add to our pleasure a delicate appreciation of sweet music.'

CHAPTER THIRTY-SIX

Since Isla had invited Jake and his wife Molly to come to stay and work at The Glasgow Bell, Jake had been intensely grateful. He was a good worker, and the customers liked him. They weren't, it seemed, in the slightest put off by his disfigured face. No doubt they had seen chrome workers before and the terrible damage that the work had done to them.

Jake was as tough as – if not tougher than – any of the navvies. Maybe that was one of the reasons why they liked and respected him.

However, Isla discovered that Jake had a secret. Jake wrote poetry. Early one morning she had found him leaning on the bar counter, busy with a quill and a sheet of paper. She had come in quietly, her bare feet making no sound on the floor, and had seen what he was writing before he had realised she was there. He was terribly embarrassed and made her swear that she would divulge his secret to no-one. Apparently not even Molly knew that he had this talent.

Isla insisted on reading the poem he had just written. She was delighted. 'I'm going to hang this up on the wall for everyone to see,' she told him.

Jake's face quivered with distress and alarm. 'Oh, please mistress, you'll be the finish of me. I'll never be able to live down the shame of it.'

'Don't be ridiculous,' Isla said. 'They'll be as proud of you as I am.'

'No, please mistress. I don't want anybody to know,' Jake pleaded.

'All right then,' Isla agreed eventually. 'I won't tell anybody that you've written it but I'm still going to hang it up. It is such a fine description of the canal.'

Jake agreed with much reluctance to allow her to put the poem in a frame and hang it on the wall. After she did so, she stood back and proudly admired it.

The poem was called 'Cargoes' and every time she passed it, she read it until she had it by heart.

Alabaster stone in lumps,
Vermicelli, brass hand pumps,
Barometers to show the weather,

Mangel worzels, barked hand leather,
Puddlers' ladles, looking glasses,
Rabbit fur and palliasses.
Sashes, frames and ventilators,
Mortar and pestles, new potatoes.
Gleaming spades, bright and bold,
Cider and perry fill the hold.

Drawn by horses, all sure-footed,
Gabberts and scows will not be looted.
Trundling daily there and back
From Port Dundas to Coney Park.
Trumpets toot and round the bend
Past Townhead the barges wend.
Bustling wharfs await their call
On the Forth and Clyde Canal.

That night when the men came in, they all read it too. Those who could not read were read to by their more literate mates. Everyone agreed it was a grand poem.

For all their roughness and ribaldry, they were proud men. Proud of their work and proud of what they had achieved. They thought of it as their canal. For them it didn't belong to the shareholders, the men of power and wealth like Lamond, it belonged to them – the navvies who had carved it out of the soil with their picks and shovels and bare hands. And in some small way this simple poem seemed to be a tribute to all their hardship and toil.

Isla had noticed how the men had acquired a pride in their work and indeed, in themselves. Nowadays they knew how to control their baser instincts. They were allowed to become merry but they knew the limits at The Glasgow Bell. They always left happy and singing but able to walk back to their bothies. If by any chance one of the men had overdone it and felt sick, he knew he had to vomit outside and well away from The Bell.

Isla had even got their urine organised to her advantage. It was a useful raw material employed chiefly in the woollen and silk manufacturers' in the making of dyestuff called cudbear. This process consumed a very considerable quantity – about two thousand gallons a day – and the manufacturing firms had fifteen hundred iron bound casks dispersed among the workers and tradesmen's houses in Glasgow and its suburbs. Isla had arranged for one firm to collect such casks from The Glasgow Bell. For each cask of urine, they paid a good price and it became quite a profitable sideline for the hostelry. Even the gentlemen's chamber pots from the gambling rooms were collected and added to the casks.

In general, Isla now believed that the navvies behaved as well as, indeed better than, many of their fellow Glaswegians and even quite a few of the so-called quality she knew. All the navvies needed was a strong hand to guide and control them. Inside The Bell she was their master, but outside its walls everyone acknowledged that David Hudson was the only man who could supply the strong leadership and discipline they needed.

One of the serving wenches even went so far as to make a light-hearted reference to the similarities between Hudson and Isla, saying, 'He's knocked the navvies into shape on the canal and you've done the same thing in here. You make a right pair.'

'Don't pair me off with him, even in your thoughts,' Isla replied angrily. But even as she did so, she knew that there was more than a grain of truth in what the impudent girl had said.

CHAPTER THIRTY-SEVEN

The wedding day was to be at the end of September. Lamond had wanted it to be earlier but Isla had persuaded him to be patient. She had a lot to settle up at The Glasgow Bell. She wanted it to continue to be successful and although Archie Anderson was no longer drinking to the extent he used to, she still didn't completely trust him to run the place on his own.

She was considering transferring her share of the business to Molly and Jake, and had decided that some time during the summer she would take a trip to Edinburgh and discuss the matter with Mr McTaggart the lawyer.

Meantime she had much business to do in Glasgow. She made regular journeys to the town to order supplies for the hostelry. She enjoyed these weekly visits, immersing herself in the vigorous bustle of the place. She had even started visiting the ladies in their flat. At first it had taken quite a bit of nerve to appear uninvited on their doorstep. After all, as part of the family, at Kirklee they had always been very scathing towards her and anything but friendly. However, when they saw that she was now in the habit of dressing fashionably and behaving with the dignity of a lady, they accepted her with comparatively good grace and began to take quite an interest in the forthcoming wedding. They advised her about the materials she should purchase for her wedding dress and her trousseau, and even made suggestions about food for the wedding banquet.

Isla was glad that their relationship had moved to a friendlier footing. Her hostility towards the family had long since mellowed. Yes, she would make a few changes. She would get her own way, but it would be by ladylike means, not by thrashing about and screaming and weeping and cursing as she once had. She realised now how different she was from the wild Glasgow urchin the old Earl had found outside The Glasgow Bell.

As she rode towards the town, she passed the new village of Port Dundas – or garden suburb of Glasgow as the wealthy merchants of Glasgow were calling it with its large villas and gardens on the banks of the Forth and Clyde Canal at Hundred Acre Hill. It was in a lovely setting and Isla could imagine many of the successful merchants leaving their crowded tenements and taking up residence here. The place had a most pleasing and lively appearance, the houses seemingly intermingled, not only with trees, but with the masts and sails of large vessels, though neither river nor canal were to be seen from Isla's viewpoint.

When she reached the streets of Glasgow, Isla felt amazed at how much trade in Glasgow had increased since the building of the canal. Far from being defeated by being deprived of the American trade in tobacco, the Glasgow merchants had lost no time in looking out for new sources and accordingly extended their commerce to the West Indies and the continent of Europe. One great loss in foreign trade was amply compensated now by the huge increase in manufacturing which promised to be a source of greater, and much more permanent wealth than the tobacco trade.

The extra work created had caused the town to expand rapidly. But alongside the fine new buildings, there was still the dark side of the town. Isla passed a whole string of poor, dirty little girls, bareheaded and barefooted, dressed in ragged and musty looking clothes. They were all trying to sell something – pieces of fruit, onions, handfuls of cabbage and cauliflower, pieces of cheese. Other vendors were pushing forward, hands offering crockery, hard and soft wares of every kind, as well as basins of little bits of broken meat, fresh or salt, bone and sinew.

In some closes and stairs, damp earthy smelling places, dark as the grave, lived thieves and prostitutes who had sunk into depths from which they would not rise again. Disease and death would inevitably overtake them and, like thousands before them, they would pass away unremarked into forgotten graves.

Isla felt intensely grateful that she had been saved from such a fate, first of all by being taken to Kirklee by the old Earl, then by making her own way at The Glasgow Bell, and finally – most fortunate of all – her forthcoming wedding to a noble lord. With all her heart she sincerely thanked God for such good fortune.

CHAPTER THIRTY-EIGHT

Isla had stayed in Glasgow much longer than she had intended. She placed her orders with a variety of tradesmen, then rode around the streets, observing with interest the many new buildings that had recently been constructed. Everywhere she looked, industry seemed to be thriving, making everything from ropes and cordage of all kinds, to soap and candles, sugar, machinery, bottles and green glass. And as for the breweries – business had never been better.

After her tour of the town, Isla made her customary visit to see the ladies. On this occasion, it turned out that they were entertaining other guests. Nevertheless, she was made welcome and they insisted that she remain for supper, which was served very late.

It was dark by the time Isla mounted her horse again and started on her return journey to The Glasgow Bell. Inns and taverns were already spilling out their revellers, and the streets were noisy with song, with groans, with laughter, and with all manner of gross obscenities. She passed black closes and wynds no more than four or five feet wide. Overhead, lit by a full moon, were lofty old houses approached by dirty, dilapidated stairs. An occasional candle flickered weakly at a window.

Isla was glad she was on horseback and not on foot. Even so, she felt uneasy and spurred the horse into a gallop. Soon she was into the countryside again and passing Port Dundas. It was not long after she had passed there that she noticed a reddening of the sky. Soon she could see quite clearly flames shooting high into the air. When she also saw the fiery reflection on the water of the canal, she was suddenly terrified that it was The Bell that was burning.

As she galloped nearer, she realised that it wasn't The Glasgow Bell. Filled with a growing sense of foreboding, she saw that it was one of the bothies in which the navvies slept. All around her, terrible screams and shouts filled the air. People were running about madly, struggling to fill buckets with water from the canal to throw onto the conflagration. The bothy itself was almost hidden from sight by sheets of flame and clouds of dense, black smoke. No-one could still be alive inside there, she thought with a shudder.

Leaping from her horse, she was amazed to see the unmistakable figure of David Hudson silhouetted against the flames as he staggered from the burning building. He was dragging one of the navvies to safety. It was Charlie, his features horribly burned and blackened, his eyes huge with pain and terror. Hudson stretched the lad out on the tow path and had no sooner done so than Charlie's eyes closed and the freckled face, which had struggled so many times and with such desperate concentration to communicate with Isla, became still. It was then Isla noticed that Hudson's clothes were smouldering. Desperately, she rushed towards him and beat out the embers embedded in his coat.

Hudson was too numbed and exhausted to notice, and he just slumped to the ground, his eyes staring blankly all the while at Charlie's lifeless form.

Isla took charge, calling out to one of the navvies, 'Help him onto his horse. I must get him to The Glasgow Bell. Put the other injured onto the cart and bring them along too.'

The man nearest to her looked distraught.

'There's only Charlie. Of the twelve that were in there, he's the only one who came out, poor laddie. And that's only with Davie's help. We tried our best to get in and save the others, but we couldn't manage it for the flames. God alone knows how Davie got in and out of there alive.'

'Oh God,' Isla groaned. 'Get a horse, ride as fast as you can to Glasgow and fetch a doctor.'

One of the navvies galloped off and the others got Hudson up on his horse. Isla knelt down beside Charlie.

'Oh Charlie,' she whispered broken-heartedly. But there was nothing she could do for him now. Hudson was hunched forward on his horse, and barely conscious. Behind her the crash of falling timbers and the roar of the flames signalled the end of the hopeless battle to save the doomed men. Isla could bear it no longer. She mounted her horse, seized Hudson's reins as well as her own, and moved the animals gently forward in the direction of The Glasgow Bell.

CHAPTER THIRTY-NINE

She thought she heard Hudson cry out. Putting on a robe, she tiptoed through to the other room. He was groaning and she hurried over to the bedside.

'Are you in pain?' she asked.

He shook his head. Mercifully, his ordeal had left him virtually unscathed. 'No. I just keep thinking of all the good men who have perished tonight. I should have seen to it that they had proper accommodation, solid buildings – not those rickety wooden bothies that could be so easily fired.'

'It wasn't your fault,' she tried to soothe him. 'You've always done your best for the men. They have a very high regard for you.'

'My best has not been good enough,' he said.

'It was an accident. It had nothing to do with you. A candle or a lamp knocked over, that's all it would have taken. No-one is going to blame you and you must not blame yourself.'

He looked at her and for the first time she saw a softness in his eyes. They were moist with suffering.

'They were my men. It's such a damnable waste,' he said.

An impulse to comfort him overcame her and she gathered him into her arms and laid his head down on her breast. 'Hush,' she said, as he repeated the words, 'Such a waste'. She knew exactly what he was feeling. It wasn't an anonymous crowd of navvies who had perished. These men had been the life and soul of The Glasgow Bell. She had been proud to call them her friends – men like Eddie, who always wore a red handkerchief round his neck and his hat at a jaunty angle. And Big Harry, with a laugh so huge it would be heard from here to Glasgow. And dear Old Ben, who was never seen without his pipe and tobacco and who, despite his long grey hair and wrinkled face, could work as hard as the best of them. At least she had the beautiful amber necklace to keep his memory alive. And then there was poor young Charlie who had loved her so earnestly.

She felt grateful when Hudson's arms encircled her and his lips met hers. Their mouths, their arms, their skin, their thighs, their two bodies merged together for comfort.

The dark silent room became like another world – a secret world, shared only by the two of them. It was a dream, completely divorced from reality.

She arose early next morning while he still slept. She started work downstairs as usual and when she went through to the breakfast room, he was already sitting there. Nothing was said about the events of the previous night. Nor did she ask him how he felt.

There was much to be done that day in preparation for the mass burial. Isla was determined to give her dead friends a good send off, she knew it was what they would have wanted – all their mates, gathered together in The Bell to drink one last toast to their memory.

Although the funeral was to be held the following day, the gentlemen came that evening for their usual gaming session as if nothing had happened.

'My dear Isla, you look tired and upset,' Lamond said when he caught a glimpse of her as he was making his way towards the gambling room. 'I wish you'd stop working here and come to Kirklee while we await our wedding day.'

'Have you not heard, my Lord?' she said.

'Heard? Heard what?'

'Twelve of the navvies have been burned to death in one of the bothies.'

'They would be in a drunken sleep,' Lord Lamond said with some distaste. 'I can only thank God it did not happen here. Come now to Kirklee, Isla.'

'I appreciate your concern, my Lord. But I have so much to do. I want to leave everything organised and in proper order before I go.'

Lord Lamond lifted her hand and pressed it to her lips.

'As long as you know, my dear, that if you change your mind – this evening, tomorrow or any day before our wedding – Kirklee Castle will be more than happy to receive you.'

She smiled at him. 'The thought gives me much pleasure. Now go and enjoy your game, my Lord, and don't worry about me.'

He lingered over her hand again before gracefully bowing and backing away, then going through to the gambling room.

As he went she felt as though she had betrayed the dead. Why had she not spoken up for them when Lamond had dismissed their tragedy with such callousness? She began to wonder if she would have to spend the rest of her life meekly agreeing with opinions and actions she despised.

In the long bar room, the men, grouped around the crackling log fire, were unusually quiet. Nobody was crowding around the bar as they normally did, loudly and jovially ordering their drinks. It was so quiet that Jake, having completed his work in the cellars, was hunched over the far end of the counter, scribbling away. If questioned, he would claim that he was writing out an order for spirits. On the pretext of wiping the bar counter, she glanced surreptitiously along at him. It occurred to her how misleading outward appearances could be. Jake's body was hefty and plodding, like a great Clydesdale horse. Hairy arms protruded from the rolled-up sleeves of his shirt. He had a shaggy mane of hair on his big head and a repellent face half-eaten away. But hidden inside was a tender, poetic soul.

Isla turned away and went back to the kitchen. A hot and flush-faced Molly was taking the last batch of bread from the oven.

'We've had a long day,' Isla told Molly, 'and we'll have a longer day tomorrow. I'm going upstairs to bed and you should do the same, Molly.'

'Aye, I'll no' be long. I've just to clear up here,' Molly said.

On the upstairs landing, Isla hesitated outside the door of the room in which Hudson had spent the previous night. She listened but could hear no sound. Eventually, very quietly, she eased the door open a crack. The bed had not been touched since one of the servants had made it up that morning.

Closing the door again, Isla went across to her own bedroom. Exhausted but somehow still unwilling to go to bed, she went over and stood for a time gazing from the window at the sleeping canal. A pale moon glimmered on the water.

She could see logs lashed together that earlier had required two horses to draw them. A steersman standing on the raft and two men on the bank, each with boat hooks, had kept the raft off the sides of the canal. The journey between Grangemouth and the city sawmills in Glasgow, or another sawmill near Maryhill, was a long one and the horses needed to be well rested.

As she stared at the canal, she couldn't help thinking about the men who had died. They had been among those who had made this stupendous feat of engineering a reality. They had worked away with their picks and shovels day after day for a pittance. Often the fields and hills had echoed with the sound of their voices. Now they were gone. And although others would take their place, she had a melancholy feeling that somehow things would never be the same again.

Isla awoke early the next morning just as the canal was coming to life. She could also hear the chatter of the serving wenches as they descended to the kitchen to enjoy their breakfast before starting work.

She washed as best she could with the jug of cold water and the basin that stood on the small marbled-topped table. From The Bell, only Isla and Jake were going to follow the coffins to the churchyard. Molly and the other servants were going to be busy preparing the funeral meal.

Eventually, they set off on horseback to meet the cart on which were piled the twelve coffins. Isla immediately saw Hudson mounted on his horse at the head of a procession of navvies on foot. She could hardly believe her eyes, there were so many of them. Navvies from all over, hundreds of them, had come to join the mourners and pay their last respects, filling the countryside in a slow-moving mass of silent grief.

CHAPTER FORTY

Isla hadn't seen Hudson for some time after the funeral. Many of the navvies had also been absent from The Glasgow Bell. She had heard that they were all working at furious speed to finish the canal at its terminus at Bowling, a few miles further down river. This had been chosen as the western end. There was to be a grand opening at which there would be the symbolic pouring of a puncheon of water brought from the Forth at the eastern end, into the Clyde.

An Act of Parliament had been passed to enable the company to extend the Glasgow branch to Port Dundas, linking it with the Monkland Canal. This canal had been built to bring coal from the Lanarkshire coalfields to the ever growing population of Glasgow.

Isla looked forward to the opening in Bowling. As well as all the excitement of the actual ceremony during the day, great celebrations were planned to take place in Glasgow later in the evening in Stockwell Street.

Lord Lamond was not going to be present. He had to go down to England on a matter of business in connection with his late wife's estate. He had wanted Isla to accompany him but she had declined.

'I will hardly see you there because you will be attending to your business. I prefer to leave the visit to some other occasion after we are married.'

Lord Lamond had agreed with good grace. He was a charming man who always treated her with gentlemanly concern and good manners. She remembered how even while his wife had been alive, he had shown her only politeness and consideration.

Seeing the way the land lay, his servants had finally changed their tune. Whenever she visited Kirklee Castle now, she was treated with civility and respect. As far as the family were concerned, Isla had forgiven them for their previous behaviour. After all, looking back, she had to admit to herself that at times her behaviour had been wild. Perhaps she hadn't always deserved to be treated like a lady.

Now, however, her determination, her steely self control, and her expensive fashionable clothes had won her the approval of the family. She had even told the twin sisters, Lady Agnes and Lady Murren, that once she was married and installed as mistress of Kirklee Castle, they would be most welcome to return and make their home there.

They had thanked her and kissed her, but then Agnes had said, 'We've become rather fond of the town of Glasgow, Isla, and our cosy wee flat here. And we've made so many good friends among the Glasgow people.'

'Aye, that's right,' her sister Murren agreed. 'I don't think we could consider for a minute being shut away in a gloomy old castle again.'

Isla had laughed. 'Shut away? You weren't shut away, you were perfectly free to come and go as you liked. And I've never thought of it as being gloomy. Nor did I ever feel a prisoner there. I had a very happy time. At least,' she added, 'while the old Earl was there.'

Murren sighed. 'Aye, we know what you mean. We missed him as well. It's sad to think he passed away so tragically.'

'I'm surprised that Harriet hasn't returned,' Isla said.

'Och, I'm not,' Agnes laughed. 'I always thought that lassie was meant for the convent. And there's enough of them in Rome!'

Isla had met the Dowager only once since she'd gone to live in the Borders. She had come to stay for a few days at Kirklee Castle and to see little Theresa and to check that she was being properly looked after. While she was there, the Dowager paid the ladies a visit, and it was during that visit Isla had met her. She had been somewhat cool to Isla at first, but had thawed almost completely before Isla bid her goodbye again.

273

Partly because in answer to the question, 'You'll make sure that the bairn is always well seen to?' Isla had said truthfully, 'I will make sure that she is always loved and cherished. She is such a beautiful child.'

On the next occasion Isla had spoken with the ladies, they had told her that the Dowager had been much impressed, not only by her sentiments but by the improvement in Isla – in her speech, in her ladylike manners and her smart appearance.

Isla had been very gratified by this. Once she had returned to The Glasgow Bell, she had studied herself admiringly in the piers glass. This feeling was compounded by the dressmaker who was now paying regular visits for fittings and discussions about Isla's wedding dress and trousseau.

'Oh mistress, you've such a beautiful slim figure,' she kept saying. Or, 'What lovely long auburn hair you have, and such a gloss to it too.' And, 'Just look at that lovely creamy skin. I've never seen the like of it.'

Isla always laughed and shook her head, and tutted at the woman. Nevertheless, it was very pleasant to be showered with such compliments.

She had ordered a rich brown riding coat to wear at the grand opening of the Canal. Under it she wore her cream dress, and a large cream hat decorated with long cream and brown feathers.

When she was ready to leave for Bowling, she twirled around several times admiring her new outfit in the long glass. It was important to make the right impression in front of all the dignitaries who were sure to be present.

Bowling itself was a mass of people and by the time Isla reached the place where the opening ceremony was to be held, her horse could hardly move for the jam of other horses and carriages, and the crush of people on foot.

Various dignitaries and officials were already in position on the platform that had been erected so that everyone could see what was happening.

Hudson was also there, looking most impressive in his black cut-away tail coat with its high collar, his short double breasted waistcoat, his high neck cloth, his tight breeches and top boots. Shortly after the proceedings began, he was also called upon to speak.

'My Lords, Ladies and Gentlemen,' he began, 'the Forth and Clyde navigation is an enterprise, the mere concept of which would formerly have excited ridicule. But men of vision and ambition have made that dream a reality. Thirty-five miles have been hewn through rock, quicksand and moss, carried up precipices and over valleys thanks to hard work and meticulous planning.

'Thirty three bridges span its banks. It has crossed rivulets and roads, as well as two considerable rivers. Over the river Kelvin we have thrown a bridge of four arches, across a valley two hundred feet wide and sixty five feet deep.'

At this point the crowd applauded enthusiastically, and it was some moments before Hudson could continue.

'These are magnificent achievements by any standards, and I am sure posterity will marvel at what we have achieved. We are now entering a new era, my friends, and the bold venture we are gathered here to celebrate today is, in some small way, a symbol of that future. A future in which commerce will thrive, and the old discredited ways that have held back the march of progress will be overthrown.'

Here Hudson was interrupted once more, but this time by the murmurs of disapproval emanating from both the ladies and gentlemen in the crowd and certain of the dignitaries on the platform itself. To them, this sounded like dangerous, almost revolutionary talk.

Hudson pressed on, 'Fear not, gentlemen! I do not seek to ferment the kind of discord and conflict we have seen elsewhere. If there is to be any talk of revolution in this land, let it be of an industrial and commercial revolution! A revolution that brings not bloodshed and suffering but prosperity for one and all! The success of this venture has shown what can be done, what it is now in our power to achieve. We cannot, must not, turn our back on the future and the incalculable benefits that it will bring to us all.'

Hudson's bold oratory had once more won over the crowd, and as he sat down they cheered wildly, throwing their hats in the air and crying out 'Bravo! Bravo!' As he sat there, Hudson was sure that his father would have been proud of him had he lived to see this day.

After the ceremony was completed, the mass of people turned towards Glasgow and the Saltmarket, eager to enjoy the pleasures and excitements of the fair.

Isla was carried along with the mob. All around her coachmen were whipping people out of their path. At one point, fearing that her horse would be injured, she had to take her own whip to some rowdy youths. Even so, she was unable to stop her terrified horse rearing up, but just as she was about to lose her balance Hudson's big hand suddenly clutched at the reins and steadied the horse. At the same time, he gave sharp orders to the over-boisterous young men milling around her.

'I could have coped with them myself,' she told Hudson.

'I have no doubt you could,' he said, reining his horse aside to rejoin the men who had been his companions on the platform.

The journey to Glasgow ended in Stockwell Street where the fair was to be held – Stockwell Street ran parallel to the Saltmarket, both streets leading down to the River Clyde.

There, at least a dozen painted Jezebels were dancing around shamefully showing their bare legs. In the many gaily painted booths all manner of extraordinary attractions were on display – including giants and giantesses, fat boys and fatter girls, learned pigs and unlettered dwarfs. The noise and clamour which issued from comedians, tragedians, clowns, drums and trumpets was deafening, as jugglers, thimble riggers, card sharpers and a human brute who was skinning as many as twenty rats with his teeth in so many minutes kept the crowds utterly enthralled.

For a time Isla enjoyed the spectacle and the excitement of it all, except the man with the rats, but at last she decided to turn her horse and head for home. She left the crowded streets behind and, in the fading light of the summer's evening, was enjoying the peace of the countryside when suddenly she heard the clopping of another horse's hooves behind her.

It was Hudson. He came alongside her. 'I've missed you,' he said.

She thought she hadn't heard him properly. 'What?'

'I've missed you. Oh, how I've missed you,' he repeated softly.

CHAPTER FORTY-ONE

She didn't know what to do. Her heart was pounding in her chest. She wanted him to go. She didn't want him to follow her into The Glasgow Bell, but his magnetism was so powerful, it drained her resistance, her ability to think of the consequences.

They went upstairs together, not saying anything. By the time they reached the privacy of her bedroom, she was nearly fainting with excitement and anticipation. The runaway rhythm of her heart was all but choking her as Hudson began to undress her.

'I'm mad,' she thought. 'This is madness.' Yet still she eagerly surrendered to the madness.

He swept her off her feet and carried her naked over to the bed. There he took her with violent urgency, an urgency that she responded to with equal violence, clutching and clawing at him until she was exhausted.

Afterwards she wept and said, 'Why are you doing this to me? I was so happy before.'

'Why do you keep saying that,' he said.

'Because it's true,' she insisted.

'You would never be happy with Lamond. You do not love him.'

'Maybe not,' she cried out, 'but I respect him. He is a true gentleman.'

'Isla,' Hudson said, 'it's time you faced the truth. You do not belong in Kirklee Castle.'

'How dare you insult me by suggesting that I am not good enough to be mistress of Kirklee!'

She struggled out of the bed and clutched her clothes against her. 'Get out of here at once!'

He sat up, pulled on his breeches and boots and shrugged his broad shoulders into his shirt and coat.

'Is that the be-all and end-all of life for you?' he said, with an edge of bitterness to his voice. 'That society accepts you as a lady?'

'Yes, yes, yes!' she shouted at him. 'How many times must I tell you? From as far back as I can remember, when I was in the gutter and ladies in their carriages swept past me and looked at me as if I was dirt – if they looked at me at all, or when they took their whip to remove me from their path, ever since then, every day of my life, I've wanted to be a lady and show them all that I am as good – if not better – than any of them.'

She was trembling violently with the

passion of her words.

He looked at her long and pityingly before leaving the room without saying another word.

The next day she arose early and worked hard and obsessively until afternoon, when the dressmaker arrived. This time she was accompanied by her two daughters, all carrying packages and boxes. With great giggles and squeals of excitement, the three women opened the boxes and carefully brought out a rainbow of beautifully fashioned garments.

'Everything in your trousseau is completed, mistress, and only one last fitting is needed for your wedding gown. My daughters and I agree that never in our lives have we seen such a beautiful, such a magnificent trousseau. And ah, the wedding gown! Oh, mistress, just look at it.'

It was indeed a lovely creation. Isla tried it on to the gasps and cries of admiration from the dressmaker and her daughters.

'A vision. A vision in white.'

It had a low cut décolleté that revealed Isla's cleavage and the creamy bulge of her breasts.

'Now remember,' the dressmaker said. 'Make sure that your maid does a good job on your hair. You have such beautiful hair and it is such a delightful contrast against your white skin.'

Isla didn't like to admit that at The Glasgow Bell at least, she did not have a personal maid. It was then that she decided that she must go to Kirklee a few days before the wedding so that she would have the help of the Kirklee servants to make her look her very best.

'I will, of course,' she said proudly, 'be taking up residence in Kirklee Castle before the wedding, so there will be plenty of staff to assist in every preparation.'

'Wonderful! Wonderful!' The ladies clapped their hands. 'And do remember that we will always be at your service. We will be more than honoured to make any garments that you may require as Lady Lamond.'

Isla favoured them with a gracious smile, then allowed them to divest her of the wedding gown. Carefully, lovingly, they folded it away in its box.

Isla knew she should feel happy and excited again, surrounded by all the trappings of wealth. Even with the healthy profits from The Glasgow Bell, she could not have afforded such rich garments. But Lord Lamond had insisted that he would pay for everything.

Yet at the same time, deep in her heart, there was pain. She knew it was caused by Hudson. She hated him for disturbing her so, for undermining the happiness, the triumph, that she should have been enjoying.

She hardened her heart against the pain, and tried to look forward to the return of Lord Lamond. When he arrived that evening, he presented her with a gift, a beautiful diamond necklace which he fastened around her neck. She was enchanted with it and ran to admire it in the glass above the fireplace in the gambling room.

Lord Lamond laughed. 'You are obviously pleased with my gift, Isla. I am so glad that you like it.'

'How could I not like it, my Lord? It is so beautiful.'

'Not as beautiful as you, my dear,' he replied gallantly.

She laughed and gave him a little curtsey. 'I thank you, kind sir.'

Just then some of Lord Lamond's gentlemen friends arrived in the room, ready and eager for their gambling session. Isla welcomed them warmly. Then as they were settling themselves at the tables, she called Lord Lamond aside.

'My Lord,' she said, 'I have been thinking about your invitation to come to Kirklee and remain there prior to our wedding. I would like to come next week, if I may.'

'Certainly, my dear,' Lord Lamond said. 'Just let me know when you wish the coach to call for you.'

'Very well. Enjoy your game, my Lord.'

She left the room, fingering the necklace

at her throat. Forgetting for a moment her ladylike dignity, she ran through to the kitchen to show it to Molly and the rest of the servants.

All the women squealed their admiration and excitement so loudly that Archie and Jake came hurrying through from the bar room to see what was causing all the commotion. They too admired the necklace.

Archie said, in an awestruck voice, 'That must have cost a fortune. You're a very lucky lassie, aren't you?'

'Yes, I am,' Isla said, as if to convince herself as well as the others. She *was* lucky. She wished that her mother could see her now – her poor mother who had suffered so much deprivation in her life. Her mother who had worked so hard for so many years, with no reward at the end of it. She would be so pleased and proud of her, Isla thought.

She kept the necklace on when she went through to the bar room. Hudson was there, drinking with one of the engineers. His dark eyes fastened on the sparkling jewels at Isla's throat. Then he looked away with what seemed to Isla to be distaste. He continued his conversation with the engineer and completely ignored her for the rest of the evening. On several occasions, she noticed that Hudson and the engineer raised their glasses to each other. On another occasion, they raised their glasses towards the group of navvies in the bar, and the navvies raised their tankards in response.

They were still congratulating themselves on the completion of the canal which had now joined sea to sea, from Grangemouth near Edinburgh, to Bowling near Glasgow. It was a huge achievement for which they deserved to celebrate and to be congratulated.

But somehow, as far as Hudson was concerned at least, his pride and his self-confidence irritated her. She knew she was being unfair and was more annoyed at herself than Hudson or anyone else. Why was it, she thought, that when Hudson was around all her emotions were thrown into turmoil? How different it was with Lord Lamond. She was always so cool, calm and collected in his company. That was what she wanted. She didn't want the pain that she felt when David Hudson looked at her. And now the desolation she was suffering when he did not.

CHAPTER FORTY-TWO

In her efforts to get everything organised before she finally left The Glasgow Bell, Isla took Molly and Jake into Glasgow to show them how and where to order the goods that were needed for the running of the place.

There was quite a regular trade now in breakfasts, and often suppers too, for travellers, some of them en route from England. The gentlemen in the gambling rooms also enjoyed Molly's cooking. More and more drink was being consumed too, especially port, which seemed to be fast replacing ale and even claret in popularity.

Once they arrived in the town, they stabled their horses and continued on foot. It was a pleasant sunny day and Isla, as well as Jake and Molly, enjoyed the energetic bustle of the place.

'One thing that has to be said about Glasgow,' Isla remarked to her two companions, 'it's never dull, is it? Nor listless?'

'Aye,' Molly said, 'and usually you get a good laugh at somebody or something or other.'

But the riot they got caught up in later in the day was to be no laughing matter. A mob, suspicious that anatomy students had rifled bodies from the graveyards in and around the city, were intent on smashing the windows of the university in the High Street. It had been common knowledge for some time that students made it their business to find out where burials were to take place and, no matter whether the graveyard was in town or country, they would make an attempt to remove the body. In university cities, the graveyards were regularly plundered by students and freshly interred bodies removed under the cover of darkness to the nearest laboratory. They usually refilled the grave with earth so that no evidence of any disturbance was obvious. Then after having successfully carried out a raid, the resurrectionists, as they were known, would visit a tavern or a tripe house to celebrate.

The difficulty the authorities faced was catching them in the act of committing their crime. On this occasion, however, someone must have been caught red-handed. People were shouting and shaking fists and throwing stones at the university, breaking every window that they could reach. The riot was only quelled by the arrival of the militia.

'Well, that was a bit of excitement we could do without,' Isla said.

Molly shook her head. 'I can't understand it. These young men come from good homes. And yet they go about doing things like that. Desecrating graves and cutting up folks' dearly departed loved ones.'

They decided to repair to one of the taverns to have a few drinks to cheer themselves up and by chance they chose a tavern where a crowd of customers were singing merrily at the top of their voices,

Old bachelors there strutting away,
Laughing and chatting with maidens gay,
And sorry old maidens too you'll find,

287

With their little lap dogs trotting behind.
There are sailors with blue jackets so gay,
With wenches they are marching away,
Bragging how they can steer and fight,
In Saltmarket Street on a Saturday night.

Everyone, including Isla, Molly and Jake, joined in with the chorus.

If you doubt the truth of what I say,
And wish to prove it in any way,
Just go yourselves and take a sight,
Of the Saltmarket Street on a Saturday night.

At last it was time for them to collect their horses and ride home.

'Soon,' Isla told Molly and Jake, 'we must pay a visit to the lawyer in Edinburgh and have a contract drawn up making the pair of you partners with Archie in The Glasgow Bell.'

'Oh, mistress,' Jake said. 'As if ye havnae done enough for us already! It was a happy day and a lucky one when I first set eyes on you that day in Edinburgh.'

Tears came into Molly's eyes. 'How can we ever thank you? You've been so good to Jake and me.'

'It's no more than you deserve. You've been a grand help to me and you work harder than anyone else I've ever seen. Just go on taking good care of The Glasgow Bell.

See that it keeps its good reputation and mind you keep your eye on Archie and don't let him slide back into his bad habits.'

'Don't worry,' Jake said, 'we'll see to Archie all right. But the man's been very good of late. It's a long time since I've seen him drunk and incapable.'

Thinking of their proposed visit to Edinburgh and what she intended to accomplish there made Isla suddenly feel sad. There was such a finality about it. For all practical purposes, it would end her association with The Bell. She gave herself a shake and tried to be more optimistic. It might be an end to one part of her life, but it meant the beginning of a completely new life – a wonderful life, that at one time would have been far beyond her wildest dreams.

Hudson did not appear that evening, but the next day he did arrive to join the gentlemen in the gambling room. At one point during the evening, Isla was surprised to see both Hudson and Lord Lamond emerge and signal to her to come over to them. She followed them into the empty breakfast room in some puzzlement.

Then Lord Lamond addressed her in a slightly amused tone.

'Mr Hudson tells me that you care very deeply for each other and that it is *he* that you truly want to marry.'

'Oh,' Isla cried out in exasperation and stamped her foot in anger. 'How dare you?' she cried out to Hudson. 'How dare you interfere in my life like this?' Then she turned to Lamond, 'Surely you cannot believe him?'

Lamond turned to Hudson. 'You would agree, would you not, Mr Hudson, that we are both good sportsmen?'

Hudson nodded.

'And as I am sure you have witnessed on many occasions,' Lamond continued, 'I am a good loser. The question is at the moment, sir, are you?'

'Lamond,' Hudson said in a low voice as if trying very hard to keep his temper, 'what I have told you is the truth. The problem is that she is a damnable stubborn woman who cannot face the truth.'

'Stubborn!' Isla cried out. 'He talks about stubborn. I have never in all my life known such a stubborn man. He just will not give up. I keep telling him, my Lord, over and over again I keep telling him. It's *you* I want to marry.'

Lord Lamond shrugged and smiled good-humouredly at Hudson. 'My dear Hudson, I think that we should both take the word of the lady. It's her decision. Let us go back to the gaming tables and forget the foolishness of this episode.'

Then his eyes acquired a humorous twinkle. 'I believe, Mr Hudson, I also have the advantage of you at the card table.'

Isla felt angry with him now. Foolish episode indeed! It was a lot more than that. She was furious with both of them. Damnation! Damn men! Damn the lot of them!

CHAPTER FORTY-THREE

Kirklee Castle seemed unusually quiet as Isla walked along the corridor and down the winding stairs from the nursery where she had seen Theresa settled for the night. The only sound that disturbed the silence was the occasional plop of a raindrop outside. One of the windows was open, allowing a moist fresh smell to pervade the air, as if grass had been newly cut.

Lamond was out attending to the business of the estate, but he would be back soon because guests were expected for dinner. She had recovered from her anger, and had decided that she would not allow Hudson to ruin her plans, her marriage, or her life. Indeed, the wedding day had been brought forward. It would not be long now until she was Lady Lamond and safely established in Kirklee for good.

In the drawing room she heard the sound of horses. She began to hurry downstairs to welcome Lord Lamond and his guests, then just in time she remembered that it wasn't considered ladylike to do this. It was the job of the maids or the footmen to open the front door and from there escort the guests to the drawing room.

Isla turned on her heel and went back upstairs. In the drawing room she sat straight-backed and dignified to await the arrival of the others. As it turned out, on this occasion Lord Lamond's guests were not the local gentry, but a group of much travelled and sophisticated gentlemen. During the dinner party, conversation and laughter rippled easily around the room. The table was laid with an embroidered Flemish table cover and set with Famille Rose plates and Bristol Glass finger bowls. Large dishes and platters of food for the first course were arranged in three imposing rows. Down the centre was a bisque of pigeons, salads, cold mutton and roasts, and a potage of carps. The left side was set with a Quaker pudding, a paté of turkey royal, and cutlets à la mantern, grilled. The right side boasted a salmon, whole and buttered, and loaves of cheese curds. The sideboard was also laden with delicacies, including a red deer pie and a leg of pork boiled with turnips.

Isla couldn't help thinking she preferred Molly's plain cooking. She had become unused to such rich and abundant fare, and had nothing to do with the preparation of the menu on this occasion. She had no desire to be like Dorothy Lamond and interfere in the kitchen. But, all in good time, she suspected she would have to have a word with Mrs McGregor or the cook about cutting down on such sumptuous spreads.

It occurred to her then, however, that Lord Lamond might not appreciate such a turn of events. He obviously enjoyed entertaining his friends, and as a good wife, she would have to defer to her husband's desires and opinions. She sighed to herself.

The conversation, meanwhile, had turned to weighty matters. Lord Lamond was claiming that there was much truth in Voltaire's sarcastic comment that at the present time it was from Scotland that the rules of taste in all the arts came, from the epic poem to gardening.

'It is perfectly true,' one of his guests agreed, 'but don't you find, Lamond, that because of the work of Smith, Hume and Hutcheson, students are eager to come to Scotland from all over Europe? They want to study modern philosophy, political economy and natural sciences here. In truth, other countries are most impressed with Scottish learning.'

'All other countries except England,' Lamond reminded him. 'England still thinks of us as backward, treacherous and poor. They make endless jokes and references in their drama to the cunning, cringing, wily Scot.'

The guest laughed. 'My dear Lamond, we ought to take them to law. There is surely an excellent case there for defamation of character.'

Isla's attention began to wander. She lifted a sweetmeat and chewed at it absently. The ladies had begun to talk among themselves. As usual, Alice Raeburn was talking in a louder voice than most. Isla's thoughts drifted back to The Glasgow Bell. She wondered what Jake and Molly and Archie would be doing right at this moment. She wondered how many customers there would be in the bar room. She imagined the talk and the laughter. She remembered the feeling of camaraderie among the navvies. She thought of her own bedroom and the view from the window of the canal with all the life of Glasgow flowing along it. Then into her mind came a few lines of Jake's poem.

Alabaster stone in lumps,
Vermicelli, brass hand pumps,
Barometers to show the weather,
Mangel wurzels, bark tanned leather.

She wondered what would happen if she suddenly recited the poem out loud, and smiled ruefully to herself. It would not be appreciated, especially by the ladies. They were only interested in the latest fashion in gowns or some titbit of scandalous gossip.

Eventually, the ladies retired to the drawing room and left the men to their claret and cigars. 'Once I am mistress of this house,' Isla thought, and not for the first time, 'I will choose my own guests and I certainly will not invite Alice Raeburn.' Already she was heartily sick of the sound of the woman's voice and mightily bored with the general conversation. It would be different, she kept assuring herself, once she was Lady Lamond.

Meantime she managed to retain a dignified politeness and when the guests at long last took their leave, she bade them a smiling farewell. Once in the privacy of her bedroom, however, she shut the door and said out loud, 'Thank Goodness.' She felt that it had been the longest and most tiresome day of her life.

She realised she had become used to working from morning till night in The Glasgow Bell and seemed to have thrived on being so busy. Well, this was a large castle with many rooms and much to attend to. No doubt in time she would find plenty to do here too. And there was Theresa to care for. There was in fact quite a lot to attend to now. After all, the wedding was due to take place in only a few days time.

Next day, she felt slightly more cheerful.

She had long talks with Mrs McGregor and the cook, and the servants. Isla did not take a high-handed attitude with any of them. Instead she encouraged them, asking their advice and praising the suggestions that they put forward – for the menu, for the floral arrangements, and even the musical entertainment.

As each hour passed, the house became more and more lively. Everyone was caught up with it and Isla was no exception. The only exception was Lord Lamond. Nothing, it seemed, could ever ruffle his cool and nonchalant manner.

Isla had always admired his elegant poise and never more so than now. But she was beginning to feel more and more nervous and uneasy. One of the guests, Lady March-banks, had spoken of this at the most recent dinner party. She had warned Isla that every bride-to-be suffered this temporary afflic-tion.

'Believe it or not, my dear, you'll experi-ence all sorts of fears and doubts. It sounds ridiculous, I know, but believe me, you will! You will! We all have. But don't worry. Come your wedding day, all your doubts will evaporate.'

Isla, lying wide-eyed and sleepless in bed every night now, hoped and prayed that Lady Marchbanks was right.

CHAPTER FORTY-FOUR

The wedding of Lord Alexander Lamond and Miss Isla Anderson was to take place in the parish church at the Cross in Kirkintilloch. A small plain building with crow-stepped gables, the church had originally been built as a chapel to the Virgin Mary in 1644. Kirkintilloch itself was situated on the line of the ancient Roman wall, close to one of the ruined forts or peels with which it was studded.

Isla often visited the town and was familiar with its narrow, irregular streets striking off here and there without apparent harmony or design. A bridge of three arches spanned the Luggie stream, while running through the town was the silver ribbon of the canal. During its recent construction, ancient un-finished altars, a tablet and a quantity of Roman pottery had been discovered. All in all, Kirkintilloch and the surrounding countryside were very pleasing to the eye.

In the distance were the Campsie Fells and the broad and beautiful straths of the Glazert and the Blane, and the Kilpatrick Hills. Isla tried to imagine herself dressed in her beautiful white gown emerging from

Kirkintilloch church to be greeted by crowds of well-wishers at the Cross. But as each day passed, nothing was successful in calming the growing panic that she had begun to experience. There was no reason for the panic. Everything was going splendidly. Not one hitch had occurred in the wedding plans.

Nevertheless, by the eve of the wedding, Isla was convinced that she was doing the wrong thing. She kept telling herself that she was being ridiculous. Eventually, in desperation, she sent the coachman with a note to Lady Marchbanks inviting her to come for tea.

Lady Marchbanks readily obliged. She was a plump, jolly, unfashionable woman who still wore hooped petticoats. She also still favoured a high padded headdress on the front of which she perched a very large hat. Over the teacups, Isla confessed her anxiety. Lady Marchbanks laughed.

'I told you. I told you,' she cried. 'Isn't it amusing? We have all suffered the same thing, my dear. I do assure you. I understand of course that you may be experiencing more acute difficulties because you have the disadvantage of not coming from quality.'

Isla bristled and her green eyes darkened with anger. But Lady Marchbanks seemed totally unaware of Isla's sudden change of mood and chattered on quite happily. 'But you have nothing to worry about, I am sure.

You have adapted very well, very well indeed. And you have lived here before. You have no doubt learned much from the noble Lamond family. And I do assure you that none of us hold your lowly background against you. Rest assured, I and the other ladies will be happy to continue to guide and advise you.'

Isla regained her composure. She knew Lady Marchbanks was kindly disposed and meant no harm. But her words merely confirmed what Isla already knew. No matter how hard she tried to fit in with these people, to adapt herself to their ways, she would never truly be accepted as one of them. Ahead of her stretched the bleak prospect of a lifetime spent trying to prove herself every bit as good as them. And although she knew she was more than a match for any of them, did she really want to endure the genteel condescension of these people every day of her life?

'Thank you, your Ladyship,' she replied. 'I appreciate your kindness.'

Eventually Lady Marchbanks made to leave. 'Now,' she said, 'get a good sleep tonight so that you can be fresh and looking your best tomorrow. Everything will be wonderful, my dear. Now please don't worry. Promise me you won't worry.'

Isla kissed the older woman's cheek. 'Thank you again, Lady Marchbanks. Our talk has been most useful.'

Lamond was away for most of the day, and in the evening he disappeared again, no doubt to enjoy himself with his friends. Isla wandered around the long shadowy corridors of the castle. Never before in her life had she felt such loneliness.

Later, when she retired to bed, far from enjoying a restful sleep, she lay awake for most of the night feeling sick with apprehension.

Next morning, the castle was alive with activity again. Several of the maids helped her with her toilette, and the donning of the wedding garments. In no time at all, it seemed, the coach had arrived. Pulled by four smart horses, it now waited to received her.

It had called for Archie Anderson first, and he was waiting for her, all smiles and looking resplendent in his new clothes.

'A great day,' he said, rubbing his hands in delight. 'A great day and a happy day for all of us.'

Isla felt far from happy but she remained quiet and dignified.

'Oh, you look a right lady,' Archie said. 'He's been the makings of you, that Lord Lamond. A right lady you are now, there's no doubt about it.'

Isla wished he would stop chattering. She couldn't think for the sound of his voice filling the coach. Before long, they were in

Kirkintilloch and she could see the church near the Cross.

A lump came to her throat when she caught sight of the crowd that had gathered outside. It was the navvies. Hundreds of them, caps in hand, and all dressed in their Sunday best.

Alighting from the coach and taking Archie's arm, Isla entered the church. As she walked down the aisle, Lamond turned and smiled at her, but she found herself unable to smile in return.

'Oh God, oh God,' she kept thinking, 'what am I doing?'

The ceremony began. It moved on inexorably, except for the usual pause when the minister asked that if there was anyone who objected to the marriage taking place, now was the time to speak up – or forever hold their peace.

It was then that an astonishing thing happened. The church suddenly filled with navvies. They streamed down the aisle and between the wooden seats and the walls.

'We object,' their leader roared. 'Each and every one of us.'

The minister looked flustered. Nothing like this had ever happened before. Then the navvies pressed back against each other, opening a narrow passage from door to altar. At that moment Isla saw Hudson striding down the middle of the massed ranks of his men, his highly polished boots sparking on the stone-flagged church floor.

Reaching Isla but not looking at her, he addressed Lord Lamond.

'I cannot allow you to be deceived, my Lord. I have too high a regard for you.'

For once in his life, Lamond was lost for words, although he still retained his normal aristocratic coolness. Without waiting for a reaction, Hudson suddenly swept Isla into his arms and strode back down the aisle and out of the church to his waiting horse.

Isla was furious. Without even a by-your-leave, he was doing this. Without even a glance at her. He was the most arrogant man she had ever met in her life. She pummelled him with her fists and kicked her feet, revealing an immodest display of white stockings and shoes.

He, meanwhile, flung her unceremoniously onto the saddle and leapt up after her. Lashing the horse across its withers, he galloped away to the accompanying cheers of the navvies who were by now streaming out of the church.

Flushed and dishevelled, Isla twisted round to shout at him, 'Just you wait till I get off this horse and get my hands on you!'

He grinned at her, his dark eyes wicked.

'That's my girl,' he said, and, suddenly without realising it, she was smiling too.

The publishers hope that this book has given you enjoyable reading. Large Print Books are especially designed to be as easy to see and hold as possible. If you wish a complete list of our books please ask at your local library or write directly to:

Magna Large Print Books
Magna House, Long Preston,
Skipton, North Yorkshire.
BD23 4ND

This Large Print Book, for people
who cannot read normal print,
is published under the auspices of

THE ULVERSCROFT FOUNDATION